the
LOS ANGELES
REVIEW

the LOS ANGELES REVIEW

Volume 22

EDITOR KATE GALE

MANAGING EDITOR KEATON MADDOX

ASSISTANT MANAGING EDITOR DEIRDRE COLLINS

EDITOR-AT-LARGE RILEY MANG

FICTION EDITORS MEREDITH ALDER & AMY SATHER

POETRY EDITORS BLAS FALCONER & VANDANA KHANNA

NONFICTION EDITOR ANN BEMAN

ASSISTANT NONFICTION EDITOR FLORENCIA RAMIREZ

TRANSLATION EDITOR PIOTR FLORCZYK

BOOK REVIEWS EDITOR ALYSE BENSEL

ASSISTANT BOOK REVIEWS EDITOR DANIEL PECCHENINO

COPY EDITORS IAN MCELFRESH & ERIC HOWARD

PUBLISHER TOBI HARPER

The *Los Angeles Review* Is a Publication of Red Hen Press

The *Los Angeles Review* (ISSN 1543-3536) is published by Red Hen Press.
Copyright © 2018 by Red Hen Press

The *Los Angeles Review* is published annually. The editors welcome electronic submissions of fiction, nonfiction, poetry, book reviews, profiles, and interviews. Please go to www.losangelesreview.org for guidelines and reading periods. All rights revert to author on publication.

Subscription rates for individuals: US $20.00 per year. Libraries and institutions: $24.00 per year. Subscriptions outside the US add $10.00 per year for air mail. Classroom and bookstore discounts available. Remittance to be made by money order or by a check drawn on a US bank.

Visit us online at www.losangelesreview.org.

Book design by Selena Trager
Cover design and artwork by Annie Dills

ISBN: 978-1-59709-434-4

Acknowledgments: The works and ideas published in The *Los Angeles Review* belong to the individuals to whom such works and ideas are attributed, and do not necessarily represent or express the opinions of Red Hen Press, any of its advisors or other individuals associated with the publication of this journal. Certain works herein have been previously published and are reprinted by permission of the author and/or publisher.

The National Endowment for the Arts, the Los Angeles County Arts Commission, the Dwight Stuart Youth Fund, the Max Factor Family Foundation, the Pasadena Tournament of Roses Foundation, the Pasadena Arts & Culture Commission and the City of Pasadena Cultural Affairs Division, the City of Los Angeles Department of Cultural Affairs, the Audrey & Sydney Irmas Charitable Foundation, Sony Pictures Entertainment, Amazon Literary Partnership, and the Sherwood Foundation partially support Red Hen Press.

Contents

FICTION

POETRY

the LOS ANGELES REVIEW

To Our Readers

KATE GALE

I**N HISTORY, 2017 WILL GO DOWN** as the year of the woman. From the women's march to the #MeToo movement, women claimed power. Not just token power, or the power to speak up, but the power to make change in society for ourselves, our daughters, our sisters, our future. We said no to sexual predators; we said yes to our own power to fight back.

Thanks to the generosity of Peggy Shumaker and Joe Usibelli, Red Hen Press now has a permanent home in Pasadena which includes offices, community space, and a stage for performances. We are grateful for their generosity and to be part of the Pasadena community of arts and sciences. Pasadena is a city of big thinkers and makers. Einstein spent three winters in Pasadena with his wife Elsa. Pasadena welcomes change agents, and Red Hen Press is part of changing the literary landscape of Los Angeles.

This story by Ashley Farmer is the quintessential piece for this *Los Angeles Review*. We ask ourselves what story we're inside and how we can write a new one. That's the story of Red Hen, and that is the story of women who are rewriting the landscape.

Awards

SABRINA LI

Splinters in My Mouth

"Distant father, lonely daughter: It's an age-old trope, but the author's emotion comes through. I admired much about this piece—the cold precision of the images, the sanitized moments of connection, the desire to feel, to hurt."

—SIEL JU, author of *Cake Time* and *LAR* Spring Flash Fiction Award Judge

THE ONLY TIME THAT HER FATHER came close to touching her was during her annual checkup. He pressed his cold stethoscope to her chest. She stared at his fingers. Thin and white and cracked from rubbing sanitizer too many times between his palms. He told her to open her mouth and pressed a wooden stick on her tongue. She watched him watch the back of her throat and wondered if he knew that she had eaten crackers and cheese by herself for lunch. He took a small hammer from his briefcase and tapped her knee with the rubber end twice. She thought about kicking him. Imagined him falling onto her. Wondered if he would be more surprised if she hugged him or shoved him. He began refilling his briefcase, putting each instrument into the bag one at a time. Before he placed the bottle of sanitizer back in, he pressed two dollops between his palms. She watched him rub away the pieces of her that clung to his skin. He closed his briefcase and left the room. She breathed out. She took the tongue compressor her father had left on the table and chewed on the end his fingers had touched until it turned to splinters in her mouth.

SAMANTHA NIEDZIELSKI

Temescal Wash & Dry

"The intimacy of the imagery resonated and lingered long after I'd left the poem. The beauty of the poem for me is in its economy—the ability to create an entire world of feeling and emotion in such a condensed space. The images are concrete, visceral and convey a very real place, at once in the real world and in the reality of memory. I appreciate how the mundane—a trip to the laundromat—can conjure something magical: an appreciation of one's history."

—T'AI FREEDOM FORD, author of *how to get over* and *LAR* Spring Poetry Award Judge

The orange cone in the laundromat reads, piso mojado.
For every sixty white tiles there is one as green
as an organic avocado grown in Michoacán, cadillac
of slippery skin and seed. Its creamy body
shaped like my abuelo's ochre knees.
My abuelo, lover of details, you raised me a poet—
taught me to fold the streets of my hometowns
under my palms like cloth napkins, to keep a letter
behind each tooth. In the foyer, we leaned upon
the lips of a fountain fashioned bare, upon
tiles you arranged like shelved soap, inventing
flowers the size of faces and kisses the size of hands,
in the water's reflection, our heads were two ceramic pots
that could laugh. I'm remembering how softly to breathe
when listening for the words panting in my chest. I am
staring at my palms, unfolding them now is to touch
myself, if only in layers. I'm beginning to recognize
this tiled paradise under my feet.

WINNER OF THE SPRING **POETRY** AWARD

One Story, Seven Times

"What I loved most about this essay was how I had to take a number of pauses while reading it so I could catch my breath before diving into the next sentence. That's how beautifully intense this essay is. And it's not just the story being told that is intense. Yes, it's a story about loss and suicide and what haunts us, which is interesting in and of itself, but the author does more than just narrate a harrowing event—she makes us experience it with her. Thanks. Using a nontraditional structure, we are shifted around different aspects and perspectives of this story, looking at all of these pieces of what was left behind when tragedy happened. This structure and the author's unrelenting prose create a force of an essay that says so much about who we are as humans and how we connect with one another, but in such a small number of words. It's a whirlwind of a story funneled down into remarkably poetic prose."
—**CHELSEY CLAMMER**, author of *Circadian* and *LAR* Spring Nonfiction Award Judge

1. In Seven Paragraphs:

I was driving to the lake when I heard the impossible news that you died in Saigon in the early hours of the morning. There was no question of intention or the possibility of an accident; you left a note.

Your funeral was this morning outside of Washington, DC. I didn't attend. I could not face your mother pouring coffee into the fine China teacups and people standing around watching the home videos from family trips to Africa and Wyoming. Besides, I've already seen all those movies.

I'm alone at my lake house in Michigan. I open a bottle of Scotch, pour two glasses and walk to the end of the dock. I sit, dropping my feet into the water. Once, we sat in this exact spot, folded into each other, eating summer cherries we bought at the fruit stand in town.

I found an old photo in my drawer this morning: a black and white strip of four snaps. In one, you are looking at the camera and I am whispering something into your ear. You're smiling. In the next two, we're looking at each other. In the last, we're kissing. Along with it, I found a small rectangular envelope from a time you sent me flowers. I opened the card and it read simply: "I miss you."

We gave each other books as gifts with inscriptions scrawled across the interior pages. My books remain filed on my bookshelf up here, still. I wonder where your books are now, the ones with my handwriting inked out across the open expanse of the title pages.

I remember the first book I gave you. I remember the last book you gave me. Your final inscription read: "The stories of our lives are braided together. For now and for always."

There are supposedly seven narrative conflicts in the stories that humans tell. Of these struggles, the human heart in conflict with itself is a cornerstone, the oldest story of them all. In this moment, I did not understand this yet and ten years later, I am still trying to figure it out.

2. In Seven Sentences:

One summer night in Saigon, your foot makes the deliberate move to step off of your seventh story balcony and then, you fall.

The blunt stone slap of the sidewalk below is the sucker punch that breaks your body.

Your soft mouth splits open wide, but no words and no answers are left to spill out.

An ocean away, the news crawls slowly and when it catches up, it catches me by the throat and I choke on my tears.

I ask: Why, Landon?

I ask: Did you feel anything, my love?

I answer: I hope, the fuck, not.

3. Our First Seven Months:

The first time I saw you, I was walking across campus. You had wild hair. You wore thick, black glasses. You were a light all your own. My gaze lingered, my eyes following until you moved out of my sight.

By graduation, we lived together. We had a small balcony and a *New York Times* subscription. You read even more than I did; your books were stacked like slim towers on your side of the bed. If I close my eyes, I can still recall our small, shared space.

After college, we eventually went our separate ways. A Fulbright Scholarship whisked you off to Asia to explore the oral histories of the Ho Chi Minh trail by motorbike; I went to New York to work at a magazine.

4. In Seconds:

From the height of seven stories up a building, an object falling to the ground takes five seconds until impact. Give or take.

One-one thousand.

Two-one thousand.

Three-one thousand.

Four-one thousand.

5. Seven Years After We Met:

My final memory of you is the Rhode Island wedding of our closest friends from college. We had introduced them. He was your best friend and she was one of mine. A happy ending did come out of our relationship. It just wasn't ours.

The wedding band played a song that struck a memory for us. You reached out your hand for me. As we danced, we watched the bride and groom and you kissed me, tenderly, on the cheek.

You said you were planning to return to the states, that Dartmouth Business School was next on your to-do list. I said that I had just started working on a book. The morning after the wedding, you left for your home in Saigon.

6. Seven Sentences, Again:

I sip my scotch and stare out into the darkness.

The water lapping against the dock and the sounds of my breath are the only noises in this still night.

I slide a finger slowly down into the drink I poured for you, swirling it in clockwise circles.

I say into the night: Landon, why?

I say into the emptiness: I tried to understand your struggle and the demons of your depression.

I admit: I guess, I never really could.

I begin to cry, exhausted, weary, wishing you the peace that you longed after.

7. Seven Words.

Only this, I still miss you too.

Parting Shot

"I love this story for its quick and slippery wordplay and how the logic of language intoxicates the story, twisting it in directions that surprise and startle. But even more than it's quickness, I admire the story for its intelligence and moments of earned wisdom that bring the story to an abrupt halt and make me sit, for a few seconds, with a difficult truth. One of those moments comes when the narrator leaves the party she's attending and drives an often-flooded road alongside the sinister-sounding Witch Creek: 'They say a witch makes the creek flood, because of course she does, a woman alone in the woods ruining things for men, making the world dangerous. Never mind how close to the riverbank some man paved the street.' The narrator of this story is often like this witch of legend. She's isolated, bereft, alone in a wilderness of men, taking the blame for their indiscretions, all the while they bring ruin down on themselves. Though grim as this sounds the story doesn't fully give way to darkness. 'There's electricity in this snow,' the narrator says, 'I wonder how I haven't felt that before?' There's electricity in this story steering it toward light."

—**BRYAN HURT**, author of *Everyone Wants to Be Ambassador to France* and *LAR* Spring Short Fiction Award Judge

THE SENATOR'S NAME IS PATRICK MALONEY but the bros call him "P-Money" and I, in my dark, private head, call him "Prick." What Prick calls me is his assistant, although I'm not it. He calls me "Twiggy" in front of constituents, orders me BLTs for lunch to "put meat on my bones" even though I don't eat meat. Today, he's lamenting a lack of old-fashioned ladies in our home state as I rewrite his memo. "A shame," he says, the big baby baiting me. He bites his pinky nail and spits it into the carpet. I keep typing, clicking, picking at the keys, sucking air, waiting him out as he paces behind me. Waiting is one of my tricks. I picture a beach where I'm swimming, kicking out into the warm blue sea. See, I'm one of the ladies he's talking about and I'm seething even though he tells me I'm sweet. Prick likes how fast I type and how I correct his mistakes without making him feel dumb. But mostly, Prick likes everything I don't.

And for me: a memo is the only thing within my control, its elegant, factual language, because I live in a windowless room with a roommate although I'm nearly too old for that now and I work sixty-six hours per week for barely more than minimum. When I'm awake, I'm awake inside a serotonin squeeze. When I sleep, it's a half-sleep filled with Prick Maloney talking at me. When I have sex dreams, they're atop mountains of memos where I wrinkle and rip edited sentences. Anger boils in my belly but I still haven't mustered the courage to refuse his greasy sandwiches that show up each day at noon delivered by a driver who earns as much as me. I chew and swallow until my body protests—something else I can't control.

What to know about Prick? He's experienced. He's a careerist. He's anti-. Prick is anti-what? You pick. He is known for passing out in his tighty-whities at night while his housekeeper cleans his kitchen and picks up his kicky novelty socks. Known for bullying. Backbiting. For a good bait-and-switch. Prick likes watching the blood drain from the bros' faces even while they ass-kiss him. Little Prick is actually big, and when he paces behind me he reminds me of my dad.

See, Prick says he wants to watch out for me.

Prick warns me to stay away from the bros.

Prick says, "Trust me, I once was one."

Prick swears a BLT tastes better with pickles and when I tell him pickles make me sick he tells me they're an acquired taste, like working in politics.

But I have my own pickle this evening: my period is late and two pee-tests indicate disaster. I spit-up in the sink and think about what to wear to the work thing tonight. Then I call my sister to tell her the news. She tells me to have a drink.

See, my sister gets me. She trains horses, or rather, she trains people to ride horses, to do pony tricks and win cash prizes. It takes money for her clients to be winners, so she knows what it's like dealing with the naturally rich, the folks who arrive in the world that way. Prick had money since the day he was a naked baby. Sister and I were not raised rich. Our family would say that's relative because you can be rich in love, I guess. I'm glad Prick isn't my relative, that no one in this podunk campaign office is.

My roommate is from Beijing, stuck in this city instead of DC where we all wish to be, thought we'd be, believed our destinies and degrees would bring us. She speaks Mandarin on the phone in the middle of the night and drinks gin. Whom does she talk to and what does she tell him? All I know is that she works in policy and thinks the senator is her enemy. "Prick is a dick," she says, because she sometimes says what I'm thinking. I search out her booze beneath the sink near the bleach. I promise in my head to pay her back for it. I pour gin in a glass with some blue-flavored Gatorade and it tastes like the opposite of magic.

Hot throat, weak knees. My black dress slack around my clavicles, my bird neck. I stand in front of the mirror with the blue drink and examine my belly, try to sense a bump or flutter but of course there's none: it's too early for that. And what do I hope I'll feel besides this creeping fear? I hope to feel nothing, which is what I'll have to figure out quick, what has to happen. Our home state hasn't made this easy and neither has the senator. My heart does its flutter thing so I think about swimming in the ocean again: it would feel so strong to go away like that because I'm always strong when I swim, but instead I have this thing tonight. "Things" are what we call these work things and honestly these things could be anything. Mostly it's small-talking with the people who do pony tricks.

Prick opens the donor's door, lets me in. See, it's not even his house but he acts like it is, says, "Welcome," like it should be my privilege. That's so him. So what I've come to expect. He takes my jacket but then a housekeeper arrives to grab it. I always have more in common with the help at these things, which is probably why the senator never brought me to his office in DC though he promised he would when he hired me.

The room is filled with the bros and the bros are filled with bravado. They half-love the senator, half-despise him. I imagine most of them think, Why not me? and the more idiotic ones think, Soon, it will be. Their cologne fills the room. Their bowties look alike and they've finally stopped noticing me in the office, the only woman in their orbit too familiar to be visible. Okay, bros. Fine by me, I think. I go from dim room to dim room, walls covered in art and books—flowers, horses, more horses, southern history with cannons and slaves—and I thread through clusters of loud men in search of the ladies and there are few of them. Most huddle in the kitchen, all of them polished and expensive and thin. Oh, their perfume. Oh, their luxury, even the sad ones, even the bored ones, especially the bored ones, like the hostess who tells a story about her kids sneaking scissors and cutting each others' hair. She picks at this bouquet and it looks like she's fixing it but there's nothing to fix. I never learned the names of flowers but these are elaborate and white, huge like anemones. I can practically hear them breathing like they're alive right there even though they're actually dying.

An hour tops, then I can leave this thing. That's another of my tricks: watch me disappear like the magician's assistant.

■ ■ ■

Want to know a secret? The secret is that Prick doesn't remember me, my parents dropping me off, my slippery feet. Me padding barefoot through his kitchen trailing Cherry, his daughter, who went to the rich brick high school named after one of her ancestors. Cherry whose mom had custody and who barely ever stayed with him. Me dripping water in a bikini, getting the tile wet. Me using the good towel with silver threading. See, they had a private pool where I would swim with Cherry and her hair swirled while she kicked like a mermaid. We raced and I was quicker. Quickest. I tried to teach her all the strokes: breath, back, side, but she didn't care. I tried very hard at things and Cherry would laugh and sing, never bothering.

Except one night I dared her while her dad slept on the black leather couch near the TV. I didn't know Prick then except that I knew he was important, which interested me. He had no pants on, which made Cherry blush but I brushed her hand as we slipped through the sliding glass door so she knew she didn't have to feel silly. It was all silly anyways: the bottle of limoncello, that other liquor that tasted like licorice and made us dizzy.

We sucked it down and tossed the bottles in the shrubs filled with lightning bugs.

Our backs. The grass. A locust summer and hotter than hell when you can hear the bugs buzz like telephone wires. Our cheeks were red then, I guess, and Cherry dared me back and said, "Naked, unless you're chicken." I'll do most things people ask, so I left my suit on the concrete, steered clear of the pool lights. Cherry said, "You're lucky you're so skinny." Cherry with her blond hair swirling. Then she kissed me, then I kissed her back, and then we raced and she never could catch me, not even laughing on the lawn, not past the dark hilarious shrubs, not at the trampoline where we laid down and the moon floated and we talked inside it until dawn.

But the senator caught her one day—with a girl, with booze, probably both, none of us knew—and then there was no more Cherry at her fancy school, at any school, not at the mall food court in the afternoons, not anywhere in our town. Instead, there were rumors of a Swiss boarding school, of rehab, of cruise ships where they make you do Christian chores until you turn straight and repent.

So what's the moral? There never was one. But her absence taught me about living invisibly since Cherry wasn't very good at it but girls like me could be. So I did, tried at least, keeping my secrets hidden under the bed, in the backs of cars, in the basement closet where no one might notice. Because if there's anything worse than being an invisible woman, it's being found out, getting caught. Red letters and all. Being seen.

■ ■ ■

Outside this donor's expensive windows the rain is hardening into snow: I can feel it in my bird bones. I think about calling someone, anyone, to confess about the pee-sticks, to tell them it was one of the bros though I don't know which, but that I know what has to happen next. It's not logistically easy and I'll have to miss work and the seconds are ticking and the weather is turning, snowflakes landing in my coat collar, melting on my neck as I walk to the car.

They say not to drive the short road along the long river because it floods almost nightly, on time like a clock. But it's the faster route and I am fast and I have to be at work again in nine hours, so I drive it anyway. It's called Witch Creek, this road, which everybody knows even though there's no sign for it. It's a name we have here in pony country, though none of the horses are wild anymore. They say a witch makes the creek flood, because of course she does, a woman alone in the woods ruining things for men, making the world dangerous. Never mind how close to the riverbank some man paved this street.

The only difference between me and Cherry, I think, is that Cherry got caught and I didn't. Hadn't, at least. Now it's different, right now, right here in the snow blowing sideways. I'm caught. Now I feel it: this dangerous chemistry happening inside me and it is the worst thing, worse than working in politics, and so I grip the steering wheel and feel the squeeze take hold again, the dark woods pressing me on all sides, the road slick, the sky heavy up there with its weight and consequences. I grip the wheel and grit my teeth and tomorrow I will take care of things and maybe the day after that I will say "No thank you, Senator. No thank you, permanently." The road curves right then left towards home. Towards sleep. Towards more snow.

And get this: it isn't freezing water or a witch that catches me. Instead, I see an animal charge the car hard, the passenger's side, horns crushing up against the window and through. I think wild horse before I get my bearings. I think, How did he find me? I think it came toward me deliberately and my hair is pricked, my skin. Then the car is light like a leaf and there's no control for me in the world. No sound, no crash. How many times will I spin beneath this black sky? I hold the wheel like the reigns of something I'm trying to tame. Then glass, then grass, then a mess of mud and sky with so much white coming down now.

I'm not hurt the way I brace myself to be and it's so still like a photograph. I hear the dying animal breathing, but it's me. I hear his horns rattling the ground while he twists in pain, but it's the car, some piece of it settling at the side of the road. Through the brush: no deer, though he is out there. I search, but I don't want to find him. I crack branches but it's slippery. I think maybe he escaped, not too hurt. And maybe if he's down, he just needs time to rest before he gets back up again. Don't birds' brains recover when they hit glass? I remember that from biology. The world is resilient.

I call my sister. My bones aren't broken, I tell her. But there is something growing inside me.

The truck, a pick-up, swerves dipshit-quick around the curve, almost clips my crashed car, his headlights blinding me. "He," I say, because I know. "He" because in this accident I've developed a psychic ability. "He" is right, this guy in jeans, hulking, who worries over me, says he'll call an ambulance. "No," I tell him. "Really," I plead because he's not listening and because I have zero insurance. He looks me up and down as he dials, my face, my hands, my feet, and I feel like I'm on display in these lights, like I've done something wrong and a cop got me. He touches my shoulder and I brush it off, but it's just to move me out of his way and then he's down in the brush looking for the buck.

He sniffs, this guy. He smashes down the brush with his boots. Yells, "Found him!" and I picture the animal all majestic, wild, tall in this snow that's getting heavy, fat flakes that will change the landscape by morning. Then the truck guy comes back, says "I'm sorry" and I don't know why because I've done this to myself. He walks to his truck and I think Good, let him leave, let me have this peace because tomorrow is going to come. Instead, he opens the door to the cab and removes a rifle.

"Wait," I say and it comes out so loud that it startles the dark up, makes the wind kind of blow, I swear, scaring the both of us.

Whose voice was that? I think. And so I yell it again and it echoes off these woods, up the road, to the windows of the house where the bored wives and bros and even the most unkind people are being polite, the senator laughing as ice clinks in his drink. I use my mind to will the buck to run.

Get up, I think, and then I see that there is glass, little chips, spread all down the front of my coat.

Well, there are many ways to be a woman and almost all of them are in spite of something. Is it morning yet? Where is Cherry now, I wonder? We were the exact same height from the tips of our toes to the tops of our heads and now she is a woman like me in this world. I want to ask her about her exile and what her name is now. I want to ask my sister what the ponies think, if they really like performing for the people who pay for it. I want to ask my roommate who it is she tells her secrets to when neither of us are sleeping. There is electricity in this snow. I wonder, how have I not felt that before? There is electricity between my legs. There is blood. Glass and glass.

And then I realize that I haven't heard the gun yet.

And then I realize that tomorrow hasn't come yet.

Then a shot tears open the night.

I finally made it through the birds the birds

"Sometimes we are told that the shorter the poem, the stronger and more inventive the language must be. But what about the longer poem, the longer poem that thrives in an age of reduced attention and spectacular distraction? 'I finally made it through the birds the birds' is such a thriving poem. It is both dense and porous. The depth of content is built in, but so is the breathing room of form. This poem asks more of the reader than the average strong poem, the average inventive poem, and does so confidently, knowing the reader will be rewarded with 'tiny teacups' and 'two-story hopes,' a 'lakegray / sky' and a 'priest of light.' Also: 'it took a chair it / took all the took / a failure so great all / the teeth the tomorrows.' And: 'it took / a prism and the first time I saw blue.' Here I find a delicate and purposeful architecture, a poem alive, layered, vented, and irreducible."

—**JULIE MARIE WADE**, author of *SIX* and Fall *LAR* Poetry Award Judge

December 21st 11:20:45 pm

I finally made it through the birds the
birds the wings of rest the v in the sky
the treads on treads I finally made it
through the prisms I was trained to see
at 3 the pictures of Lassie shaking in
black and white the curtained haloes of
purple and red the birds the birds my
guides my sling out from the lakegray
sky leaving me to a priest of light a
port of standing the roads the crest
the pier the birds the birds I know a
reach a rule a whisper a liar the
trees the smoke the two-story hopes
the reservation of skies the door to the

aviary where I finally made it through
where it took a farm it took a chair it
took all the took a failure so great all
the teeth the tomorrows the hands so
chapped and split from cleaning fluids
I finally made it through the glass of
scotch the birds the birds flew off the
pier a whisper over the water it took
a prism and the first time I saw blue I
look back as if this were the last time I
will see these rooms the green glazes
the mustard rugs the tiny teacups and
hanging glass I made it through after
having dropped from the lakegray sky
I made it through to the aviary where
the birds flew away in a whisper and I
was left with a prism a draft in the eyes
I finally made it through after being
dropped from the sky by the side of the
road our draft at a life the whisper
the halo the tomorrows the birds the
birds the whisper of whales of
prairies the moths the windows
the dirty walls

I have looked

at prisms

I have seen

the borders

I have missed

the train

if I don't know

the sky

will not

know the sky

if I don't write

the draft

of our life

the draft

of tomorrows

will not come

Mathias said

something about

great failures

and great freedoms

so I would know

the tryst

the smile

the dead lights

the sky the sky

of so many years

the trees

the smoke

our chapter

of hands

our prism

of greens

my aviary

of birds.

DEBRA A. DANIEL

And the Dish Ran Away with the Spoon

"Red Hen loves myth and fairytale. We were built on the story of the Little Red Hen, so we fell madly in love with "And the Dish Ran Away with the Spoon." It's got thrust and song of secrets and drama, the heft and pull of transgressive love, a swirl of joy as dish and spoon find each other's sweet spot on the road.."

—**KATE GALE**, managing editor of Red Hen Press
and *LAR* Fall Flash Fiction Award Judge

ALL DAY THE CUTLERY DRAWER CLATTERED with rumors. The forks are in a tangle, heads together, tines crisscrossed. The Knife's friends say he's keeping a stiff upper lip, but, in fact, he's inconsolable, won't try to cut, not even butter. He spent last night drowning his sorrows in the sink. *Should've seen it coming*, he said.

The Spoon was beautiful as sterling, not gangly like those iced tea ladies, but shapely on top, slender all the way down, with that graceful curve he admired. He knew when he lived up with her she had an eye for better things. She'd never be satisfied with a stainless life. Hadn't she spent her days dipping into sugar, diving headfirst into exotic coffees? Caffeine made her jumpy, ready for action. You don't glide through that much ice cream without craving the sweet ride.

And then along came Dish—moon-faced, bigger than life—Dish, who lived in a roomy upper cabinet, not a tight, narrow drawer. He was a dresser, had a distinguished blue border, never without a flower. He'd been around.

He was no stranger to candlelit dinners for two. He had touched the private underside of a folded swan napkin. And oh, he had stories, stories to stir desire in a spoon. He knew secrets about the dark inside of the refrigerator, details on how to survive the microwave's heat, the scoop about the night the platter cracked.

Where's the happy couple now? No one knows for sure. The Soup Ladle saw them heading down the driveway. Dish on his side, rolling easy and free. Spoon already struggling to keep his pace.

JOSEPH HERNANDEZ

The Christening of the Fruit

"This little story is packed with meaning, as juicy and fat as the fruit it meditates on. I love how the narrator's fascination with the fruit his grandmother calls 'Amarillas' evolves over the course of the story into an informed rejection of his grandmother's secretive and exclusive ways, and a new vision for his own life, how he might grow his own Amarillas tree—'a grove of sweetsunfruit accessible to all.' There are overtones of Adam and Eve, of course— the tasting of the forbidden fruit, the threat of severe punishment. And the writer's imagery is arresting: the grandmother's blouses 'the color of fading paint,' the 'sounds that pass over your tongue and through your teeth like a weak breeze in the hottest month.' Some of the images—fruit and growth, chanclas and punishment, language and naming—become motifs deftly threaded through the story. It's a delicious read."

—AMY HASSINGER, author of *After the Dam*
and *LAR* Fall Short Fiction Award Judge

WINNER OF THE FALL **SHORT FICTION** AWARD

I N THE GARDEN IN HER BACKYARD my grandmother has a tree that bears a fruit that grows fat and ripe like suns. She calls the fruit Amarillas, not by its name, but by its color. It is off-limits to everyone, my family and I know; no one but my grandmother can pluck it from where it hangs because, she says, she is the only one who can tell when it is ready for harvest. She doesn't even let us help her pick it. So, because she cannot reach the lowest branches, she is left to spend hours stacking chairs, climbing the fence or swatting the tree with a rake, causing a rain of smashed fruit on the sidewalk that not even her dogs are allowed to lap up. When she has gathered enough basketsful, and there is no more yellow-orange on her tree, she takes them to the local farmers' market to sell or trade for meats and spices.

Her christening of the fruit and its aversion to an English-sounding name had never surprised me, though her creation of a brand new word had. Though my grandmother could make a meal out of anything with a root or a stem and she was no stranger to chopping the heads off once-living chickens or fish, she was not an otherwise innovative woman. She often dressed in blouses the color of fading paint and she hadn't missed a Sunday mass probably for as long as she'd lived. In naming the fruit she'd ensured that she'd avoided the soft T's and flat R's of the English language, those sounds that pass over your tongue and through your teeth like a weak breeze in the hottest month. She hated the taste of English words in her mouth, she'd always said. She only seemed to endure the language's words on her tongue when she had to speak to me.

When I was younger she would bring me to church with her. I would sit there, understanding nothing that was being said, letting my eyes wander the cathedral, digesting the browns and whites of the pews and walls, the rainbows of stained glass. After the mass, my grandmother would take me to the front of the church and kneel down before a statue of a cloaked woman. She would put her head down and say nothing and I didn't know if I was supposed to do the same. Afterward she'd buy us apples from a nearby vendor, always handing me the larger one. This was the only time in my life my grandmother would share her fruit with me. Then, one winter evening, she brought a small green stem home from a market-venture. She said she'd been looking for one of these for years now, said she hoped it would survive in the soil in her yard. When it did survive, she watered it every day as it began to sprout. And she stopped taking me to church with her.

If my grandmother had a choice between anything she owned and her Amarillas tree, there would be no contest. I might even believe she'd choose the tree over me if it came to it. Before the Amarillas grew into her life, she had a statue, a pale porcelain rendition of the Virgen de Guadalupe. One day I broke the statue. Knocked it over by accident. Caused a whole mess of Virgen-shards on the floor. When she came home she found that it was in pieces in the garbage.

"Do you want the belt or the chancla?" she yelled, then proceeded to spank me until I was too sore to cry. And now that I see how much of her time and energy she dedicates to the tree and fruit, I'd much rather not imagine what she'd hit me with if I meddled with that. If I even ate just one.

I have learned the true name of the Amarillas, though I've never told my grandmother. I was dating a girl who spoke the same language as my grandmother, would derive her words from the same roots. But this girl would not misname the fruit as my grandmother had. And I wouldn't tell her I had known of its existence before her, either.

My girlfriend liked to sleep with nothing covering her body, and she always smelled like strawberries (the fresh-from-the-earth kind, not the artificial-candy kind). Her name was Lucinda, and she told me she had a jungle in her backyard. I thought this was a joke until she took me to her home, in a part of Los Angeles I had never been to with too many intersections and too little space in between the small houses. Her backyard was as large as the rest of her house, with a shaded canopy to cover the vibrant green of plants in dark orange ceramics. And in the center of the green, beyond the vines of rosemary and a wasp's nest that hung near our heads, there was an Amarillas tree.

"What is this tree, I've never seen it before," I asked. She told me that it had been planted since before she and her family moved here, that her father tended to it like one of his own children.

"He's lucky," she stated, "A tree like this is rare and he hasn't been able to find another one since."

Then she apologized to me, amid the buzzing of wasps and a rustle of leaves in the wind. She said she wanted me to try the fruit, but that it was not yet ready: small, pale bulbs had sprouted from the leaves and would not grow in full for several more months. She told me she'd bring me back when there was fruit, when there was more color in her yard.

As we walked away she sighed and said the word, a succulent delicacy in her accent:

"Persimos."

I never asked Lucinda what more she knew. She had told me enough. I let the word drip into my lexicon, sticky like an orange in summer. I felt empowered now, knowing the true name. I felt I could go to markets and say the word, "Persimo," could whisper it into the ears of market-goers. It would be our language, a secret more accessible than the Amarillas word. I wondered if Lucinda could connect with people who also knew this name, as I felt I now could?

After she said the name I looked differently at the tree in my grandmother's backyard. I no longer understood her reverence of it. Here was a fruit with many names that even her own family was not good enough to taste. I asked her, the day after visiting Lucinda's jungle, if I could take an Amarillas. "It's just a fruit," I told her, "more will grow." She was at the kitchen sink slicing a cactus for dinner.

"They're not ready to be eaten yet. And even when they are, I will need to bring all of them to the market. I will count them all. I get paid for each one," she said without even looking at me.

"Well, couldn't you get paid for one less?"

She stopped slicing. I thought back to the days of the chancla and how she'd never hesitated to hit me when I talked back. When she did nothing I backed out of the kitchen and before I was in the hallway I heard her resume chopping and slicing, preparing for a dinner I would not enjoy that night.

On the last day I ever saw Lucinda, she was eating one. She split it open with a knife, but didn't offer me the other half. She slurped and sucked the fruit, and it was neither arousing nor obnoxious. She told me she would see me in a few months. She was going to Mexico with her family. I didn't tell her to stop eating the fruit in front of me like that. I didn't want her to leave me for that long amount of time. I wanted to shout at her, if you are from Mexico and my grandmother is from Mexico, why don't you call fruits the same thing. Instead I said nothing and watched as she spit dark, flat seeds onto a paper plate.

I first tasted the sweetness of the Amarillas with my friend Julian. We were in his room. It was summer. We were working out a dream we both had, where the two of us would start a band and leave school. He had a guitar, and I had scribbled lyrics for songs on orange construction paper. Neither one of us could sing, but I always told him he could. I liked hearing him try and hoped that eventually his voice would grow on me.

He shouted to his mother that he was hungry. She told him she was making dinner, and to find something else in the meantime. He left the room and came back with a basket of mixed fruit. I recognized them immediately. Toward the top sat two of them, gleaming and golden. He asked which I wanted and I told him to surprise me. He threw it to me and I caught and held its cold weight, ran my finger along its creases.

"What," he asked, "you don't like these?"

"What are they?" I wanted to know what his name for them was.

"My mom likes them. I don't know where she gets them." He sat next to me then took a bite of his. "Try it."

I watched some of the juice run down his neck and onto his shirt. It bled onto the collar, a light pink.

"Damn it," he said. He stood up and placed the bitten fruit on his bed, then went to his closet and pulled off the stained shirt.

I took a bite of his fruit when his face was covered. It was sweet and cold. It was wet, too. I slurped the juice to avoid being dripped on. His skin was darker than mine and he had a scar near his bellybutton I didn't ask about. His stomach muscles clenched as he pulled the new shirt over his head.

"Is the fruit good?" he asked me. He saw that I had taken a bite. He let me eat the rest of it.

We spent the afternoon writing lyrics about sweet fruit. We finished the whole basket. By the time his mother called us for dinner, we were no longer hungry, so we stayed and wrote more. I titled one of the songs "Amarillas," and another "Hungry." He didn't show interest in either of these.

When I stole the fruit from my grandmother's tree she was not home and I was not hungry. The Amarillas had been left to ripen and would not be picked for another week. I stepped outside, and when the pavement burned my feet, I slipped into a pair of old worn chanclas by the door used to swat flies during family barbecues.

Despite being immature, the fruit was larger than my hands. The branches shook as I tore one from its stem. It was bright and smooth, but it was not pale like Lucinda's, or soft like Julian's. I wondered how angry my grandmother would be with me if I ate them all, but when I bit into it, it was sour. It left a bad taste in my mouth. I chucked it at the fence and it exploded in a cascade of amarillo and pulp. I wondered what she'd do if I took the whole tree down, tore down every fiber of color that held it together. If I chucked them all at the fence, painting her backyard in the fruit's flesh. Then I'd let her dogs clean it up.

I wanted the tree gone. No more farmers' market. No more sour fruit. No more making up names for things that already have names.

But the tree would not go. It would continue to exist in her garden, continue to fill only her basket with yellow. I spit the seeds on the ground and went back inside the house.

I have imagined a reality where instead it is I who grows the Amarillas, a grove of sweetsunfruit accessible to all. Whoever wishes to take the fruit can do so without contest. I have dogs, too, and they feast on the fallen bulbs, too ripe and luscious to stay hanging on the branches. All of the men and women who visit me know the taste, know the true name. Amarillas are always on their tongues.

RENÉE BRANUM

Certainty

"There is a hazy landscape separating memory and truth. 'Certainty' lives in this space where even false memory can gain heft, if it is conjured long enough. Original in form, 'Certainty' makes us wonder how we can ever trust those narratives around which we construct our lives or if such verifiability finally matters at all."

—CAROL BECKER, author of *Losing Helen*
and *LAR* Nonfiction Award Fall Judge

T HESE ARE THE THINGS WE WERE uncertain of:

Whether, when the bandages came off, the dog's eyes would be shrunken and clouded like juniper berries, or still brown and clear, though unseeing.

Whether the persimmon tree would produce any fruit that year, or if we even cared.

Whether the man who came to tune our piano had killed himself deliberately or accidentally.

Whether my sister liked boys or girls and whether this had anything to do with her being touched inappropriately by a babysitter when she was practically still a baby.

Whether I was actually beating Ryan at arm-wrestling, or he was occasionally letting me win.

Whether or not my father blamed himself for the dog's blindness.

Whether or not my mother blamed herself for the inappropriate babysitter.

Whether or not Uncle Mark would ever wake up from his coma.

That year, we were certain of a small handful of things. We knew the proper way to kill and dispose of a spider. We knew that Uncle Mark had never been to Africa; that the piano was deeply out of tune (though our mother still made us practice); and that the dog was an expert at being blind, brushing between the furniture quick as a fish through underwater reeds. I thought to myself pretty often, "I will never love anyone as much as I love this dog," and I believed it.

When Uncle Mark finally woke up, his hair had grown back enough since the surgery that no one hesitated to hand him a mirror when he asked for one. But when he saw himself there, in the tiny pink-and-white frame of the makeup compact, all he could say was "Ay, caramba!" And we all looked at each other; one of the uncles laughed because he didn't know what else to do. And then Mark said it again, "Ay, caramba!" and we all started to titter, couldn't help ourselves. It was all he said for days, rolling his head side to side on the pillow, lifting spoonfuls of pudding all the way to his mouth then letting them plop back onto the tray. "Ay, caramba!"

Before the accident, he'd looked like Paul Newman. After: like someone who was once told they look like Paul Newman.

When he began to speak whole sentences again, his tongue seemed to get in the way. He bit it and it bled. He talked at length, sharing memories that none of us could remember: dogs none of us had ever owned, bones we'd never broken, continents we'd never been to. He talked to me about the first time I saw snow, driving to the top of Mt. Diablo and packing snow into shapes, monoliths and turrets we sculpted barehanded. I looked at my mother, mouthed the word as a question, "Snow?" She shrugged and mouthed back, "Ay, caramba." That phrase had become code between us, code for: your uncle's mind isn't quite right.

But, strangely, he remembered it all so vividly: even the purple coat I had worn, even the fact that he'd begun to worry I might get sick from eating so much snow.

To his fiancée, he said, "Remember that time we went to Africa?"

We watched the fear shiver through her and waited to hear what she'd say. She said, "No, Mark." With calm certainty she said, "We've never been to Africa." Mark's scalp showed the color of rage through the fuzz. She, of all of us, was the only one who refused to humor him and so we watched him begin to hate her.

"In Africa," he told us once, "it is so hot that people leave stones out in the sun and use them to cook on like hot plates."

"In Africa," he told us another time, "the soil and the trees and the animals are all the same color and that color is red."

"In Africa," he told us, "people go to war with monkeys over watering holes."

After weeks of this, his fiancée stopped coming to see him, returned his ring in a yellow manila envelope.

"How," my mother once asked, "could he be so convinced of something that wasn't real?"

And yet, week by week, year by year, I've become less and less certain about the snow, seem now to remember how cold my hands were, curved ice walls melting and hardening beneath. I'm almost certain of one thing Uncle Mark never mentioned: that on that day, on the mountain, I put snow into my own hair, as if anointing myself, and I cried because it burned with cold, and my scalp shrank and tightened.

Fiction

Easy Exotic

ONCE SHE THREW EVERYTHING OUT, WE thought there would be more room. I gave away a lot I wanted. Mom said, "We can get new stuff," but you can guess what happened. Our old stuff is still gone.

Except for the puffed stuffing clumped in pockets on her pelvis, Mom is loose and sunk, humiliated by the tubes tucked up her nostrils and the respirator clacking over tile, rucking up the rug. Where she walks, dust and dirt sputter up in small clouds.

I have never been so aware of surface texture as our stripped home has made me. I know now how skin can look like an organ. Sweated holes, stretching taut on bone, lumping into tumor and thickening cyst. How could the body be forgotten?

In the end, we keep only what gets used.

I got rid of my kid clothes and my Legos and my scientific calculator and my books on How Stuff Works. I sold my CD player. I helped Mom put vases into boxes. I emptied out the colored pencil ends in the jar.

Mom is a lot. Last days she stood easy, she unplugged appliances. She wrapped electrical cords round one jutted elbow. She said, "How could we possibly have this much?"

Our home looks like a week-long rental we've lived years in, by which I mean, there is not a lot on the floor or on the walls.

Nights after her aide is gone, we watch TV together. Maybe it's awful to spend so much time tuned out, but we do. Our favorite show shows real people competing against each other to come out on top. Each week contestants get stacked by ability in a hierarchy that shifts as soon as it is declared. The order is determined by a panel of four judges, one of whom changes week to week, as celebrity guests file in and out to shout about what they're up to now. The host is an aging model with an accent.

"Who do you think has had more procedures?" Mom says. "Me or her?"

The contestants are professionals. They were chosen from countless applicants. "You are here," the aging model tells them, "Because out of everyone, we have recognized something in you."

As the season goes on, contestants are shaved off for not having enough in them of the same something the judges first saw. What I learned from our purge: when you put one thing next to another thing, one of the two will probably seem less useful.

There were three of us when the specialist said we'd soon be whittled down to two. The one we lost was not the one we thought we'd lose. Sometimes that happens, a surprise elimination.

Contestants are wild when rules like these are broken. They want to believe in a divine order to the competition. They want to believe in a system that can be worked.

A week after her husband left, Mom got rid of everything but its ghost.

He had an ugly name. We should have said no to him once we knew his name was ugly. We should have been attuned to the surface, how quickly hers would become more core than any virtue, idea, experience, emotion, or preference.

I watch her sleep. Her skin rises and falls in all the wrong places.

Listen. All I can offer I am offering. I am here with her. Hear how her breath deepens when her feet are in my lap?

He is not here with her. He is a joke I make so Mom will laugh.

How else to digest what trash her husband left us? He revved his wife's steeply sloped health into a hill we could climb together. "Only a little longer," he kept saying. "We'll tough it out till the next treatment comes along."

Imagine that but in khakis. I do the voice too.

"We," I remind her. We are watching our reality TV show; an episode in which people who cut hair cut hair on camera. She has her eyes closed.

"We," I say louder, watching for movement. "What was that about?"

She shakes her head, or makes a meek gesture at it. "We who?"

"Him We."

Mom furrows herself at me. "We've just got to stay hopeful!" she says.

I say, "We won't be able to make it this weekend! We have an appointment with Dr. Guerrero Friday night!"

"Here is a support group for us!" she says. "Here is a website with a page that publishes stories like ours!"

I ask her, "Are you sad?"

On TV, a woman is trying to describe how she'd like to look if she didn't look how she looks. She holds up a photo of herself when she was twenty-five. This is what she wants in a haircut. Mom snorts, and then coughs something up. "Whaddya gonna do?"

I pass her a tissue. She holds out her hand to me. "Baby," she says, flicked wrist. "Help me sit up."

She keeps calling what she does on the couch sitting.

"Remember the suns?" I ask her.

She remembers, and smiles. "Ugliest earrings I ever saw."

"Why did he think you'd want that?"

Mom looks long before smiling in a sorta dead way. "My naturally sunny disposition."

Next week's TV preview advertises yelling. Contestant versus contestant! Contestant versus judge! Dog eat dog eat God! Mom rolls her eyes.

"Hey," I say, and it must seem sudden because she twitches like she meant to move larger. "Is a haircut something you'd be interested in?"

She looks at me like something has happened that I am too dumb and young to understand. "No," she says. "A haircut is not something I would be interested in."

We like this show. We've watched it for years, though some seasons have been better than others. On one, a guy almost died. That was before they got the whole thing down.

It was a while ago that the model published her cookbook, but they're still promoting it, and hearing her push us to want to cook how she looks when she cooks gets me tired. Salade Niçoise á la "Easy, Exotic," Coconut

Almond Snap Pea Stir Fry á la "Easy, Exotic," Soy Chicken á la King á la "Easy, Exotic."

Mom says: "I can think of another thing 'Easy, Exotic' describes."

I tell her if I hear that title one more time I don't know what I'll do.

"Easy," Mom says. She watches me bang the back of the remote against the couch arm. "Exotic."

"It won't mute."

"Don't mute," she says. "Get me the kitchen chocolate."

I get up.

"Don't get me the kitchen chocolate," she says. "Hold my hand."

A Cheerio takes another Cheerio tubing in an endless ad for breakfast cereal. Mom puts her head on my shoulder. She is picking lint off the couch. "Why do we even own this piece of junk?" she asks.

Hours past, I hear her rattle in her sleep. Our doors stay open at night. Who was it that said God doles out dollops of hardship to those with the capacity to clear their plate? Appetite is all the god we've got here, and guess what? Here is not a lot.

Here is my mom with lymphangioleiomyomatosis. Here is her cough, shrill in a brittle night. Here is her doctor, happy to tell her the rapid progression makes her unusual. Here is the dream of all those deemed individuals: be unusual. Here is my unusual mom. She will die in line for a lung.

For years the name we had for her health was declining. A too tired to go anywhere so often overdoing it take a cat nap or cut it out kinda diagnosis. A no answer, but that she asked too much of herself, onto which she added her own wry twist: "A no answer for she who asks too much."

"You've never been shy about asking," I remind her.

She says, "Would you turn that sound down?"

Once we knew what it was called, we stopped needing to call it. Enough is quickly enough when what you've got is unpronounceable. We call it LAM. Not really, that's some support group mnemonic shit. We call it why do you still have this? Do you really need to hold onto all this old stuff?

Science says only women get sick in this way: over time and invisibly. Smooth muscle proliferates until it blocks oxygen. Her alveoli won't make way, so swollen are they with extra cells. Poor prognosis for women looking to live ten years past diagnosis, poorer if caught post-pregnancy, poorest if symptoms presented too long before a diagnosis did. "New developments every day!" Dr. Guerrero promises. He prints out a study showing survival rates gone longer than ten years, with treatment. Mom tries antiestrogen therapy, oxygen therapy, sirolimus therapy. Mom breathes with her lips tightly pursed. Lungs honeycombed in cyst—Dr. Guerrero talks transplant to treat a collapse. Worst comes to worst, he'll adhere her, lung to chest, as many times as it takes to stay stuck. Mom jokes that she is literally running out of breath. I joke that she is so dense she's dying. Treatments buy time as quickly as they use it up.

The season dwindles while we track our favorites. Mom likes gay guys who yell. She is always in support of the loudest saddest man with a bleached streak, kept on to be cut out halfway for no reason we know of, but that his emotion tired everyone out. He's called Roger this time around, and talks a lot about how he was bullied in backwater Alabama till he grew up and got out.

I google photos of the host's toddler, turning two in a televised special this month. Over takeout, we talk about who might be gone by the time the special airs. Mom wrinkles, remembering when the host's baby was just a bump under an empire waist.

"I wish you could sell me," she tells me. We watch commercials for dark cars speeding through the wilderness at night.

Her husband calls us and leaves another message on the answering machine. It sounds like he's been crying. "I wish you would pick up," he says. "I wish we could make this right."

"We," Mom says.

I delete the message. Mom says, "We who?"

It's the season finale, and everything is swollen. We order Thai food, and Mom tries to make room for me on the couch.

"Sometimes I dream this theme song," she says.

In the final episodes, when shit gets down to the wire, people usually have less to say to each other. Whereas the action of earlier episodes relied heavily on interpersonal friction, contestants hunker down into themselves as chances at championship slim. How far they've come has got a name now, and it's Final. They talk to the camera as if it has borne witness to their most secret individualities, and come down on the correct side. "It's one in three now," contestants confide.

They smile wide, suddenly and temporarily assured of their worth. "It's down to one of us two."

ILYA LEYBOVICH

A Year of Rain

I T WAS THE YEAR OF RAIN, when they hopped over puddles to reach the curb and scraped the freckles of brown mold that sprouted on their ceiling. The walls of the apartment were thin as sliced turkey and they could feel the heave of strangers' lives breathing against their own. When he lay down on the bedroom floor, the crown of his head touched one wall and his heels pressed against the other.

They pretended to have blowouts for their neighbors' sake, staging arguments about ridiculous subjects.

"You swore you'd stop curling. That game is killing you!"

"I just can't stay away. I was born to sweep the ice."

"Sometimes I think you love that broom more than you love me!"

They lived in a shabby but affordable part of town, waiting for a nicer neighborhood to self-generate around them, for the laundromats and bodegas to mature into coffee shops and antiques stores like mudfish growing legs and stepping from the sea. He insisted it was the natural progression of the urban dialectic; she took his word for it and collected their receipts.

It was a difficult era for optimists, and they suffered the million daily tragedies inflicted on the hopeful. They leaned into the gray mornings as the raindrops slanted beneath their umbrellas like scissors attacking the skin. They headed in opposite directions to catch their trains for work.

At night they came home tired and wet, and huddled together on the couch, transfixed by shows like *Black Cop-White Cop Buddies* and *Hopeful Girl Employed at Fashion Magazine*, sitting silent beside each other in the hours before bedtime, until one day they unplugged the television and deposited it on the sidewalk with mutual disgust. They returned to books: she crawled into hefty nineteenth-century tomes full of French and Russian feelings, and he reread the philosophers that had inspired him in college, hoping to reinvigorate himself through a kind of intellectual Viagra.

She wore itchy sweaters and he scratched her back. She fed him grilled cheese and soup when he stumbled home wheezing. Once a week they lifted pints with friends and commiserated about the many trials of being young and poor. Once a month they went to an expensive restaurant and ordered appetizers and bread refills. They raced each other through museums, got soaked in line for discount theater tickets. They had sex on the couch, the bed, the kitchen floor (hazarding splinters) and in these ways thought they had a life. They would have been considered insane for expecting different and better outcomes from the same daily rituals had they not been camouflaged in love.

One day she pulled in the flower box from the window and sat with it in her lap, mourning the marigold dissolved under three months of continuous rain.

"Where did the sun go?" she asked.

"It's still there," he said. "It's always been there, just behind the clouds."

"How can you be sure?"

"Astronomy. Physics. The natural order of the universe."

"When you were little, did you ever get scared of the dark?"

"Sometimes."

"Did astronomy help you then?"

"But we're not little anymore," he lied. "Besides, imagine the size of the rainbow after all this is over."

She looked at him and then out the window, as if drawing a line to connect his confidence with the reality of the world drumming against them. If it had merely been a bad storm the weathermen would have given it a name because all named things fade, but this anonymous deluge, this all-invading wet, was trouble with no sign of relenting.

They let the gray infect them for a while, succumbing to the ministrations of slow creeping ruin. There was a veterinary clinic across the street, and they'd sit for hours watching people emerge without their pets, judging the ones who cried against the ones who didn't and wondering why there was no stronger word than "grief" for when a person is made less than he was.

They visited the vast cemetery on the south side of town, its once green hills now balding into mounds of mud. Their boots sank into the swollen soil as they slogged between the gravestones, which too were becoming submerged like the memories that adhered to them.

But, like the rest of us, their eyes slowly adjusted to the darkness. It was the first great shock of the rain that threw people into despair—after a while the terror passed. They applied fresh coats of paint to the walls, invested in designer umbrellas, bought triple-layered rubber galoshes. They learned to waterproof every crack and crevice with the many hydrophobic gels that hit the store shelves.

In the papers they read about the Machine, about the uncountable billions being spent on its construction so that it could part the clouds and bring salvation. Hope, that terminal ailment, flooded their hearts again.

■ ■ ■

Every day he sat at a desk staring at a screen and tapping a keyboard until he got up and ate for forty-five minutes. Then he returned to sit and tap more keys for a few hours before going home. He tried to remember the commitment he'd once made to an authentic life and the ideas that had carried him trembling with excitement across university greens. He felt he was unlike the drones around him, who cared only about their mortgages and sitcoms and the egg salad they would eat for dinner that night, while he had galaxies of thought swirling inside him.

On rough days, when the rain was violent and great buckshots of it came spraying onto his every inch so that he was a kind of cold soup when he finally made it to his desk, the old frenzy would rise up in him like bubbling magma. It would take all his energy to keep from screaming at those around him to prove they existed, to explain to him that their so-called reality was, in fact, worthy of the name. Those moments were rare now, but when they struck it felt as if he were being drawn toward a steep precipice.

She, however, loved her job. She taught history to children at an uptown private school fronted with Greek columns and the wide dignified steps of a courthouse. The students arrived wearing crisp blue-white uniforms, and their drivers spread mighty canopies over their heads to keep them from getting soiled in the two-minute journey from town car to front entrance. She felt a sharp pleasure in exploring the past, with its long stretches of ugliness punctuated by displays of human virtue, and wanted nothing more than to sink her fangs into the young minds around her.

She spoke of how great empires broke their spines on the rocks of tiny nations, of how mankind's mastery of the world was proven not in his fruitless ejaculations into outer space but in the taming of the seas, the bringing together of distant shores. She draped herself in the finery of despots and the rags of revolutionaries, acting out a vast drama on her tiny stage.

As the rains continued and the waters rose, she noticed that the wealthy children entrusted to her care started disappearing one by one. She was told that their families had booked passage on the mysterious ships berthed like leviathans in the bay, and whose gargantuan steel conning towers were now crowding out the skyscrapers in the distance.

She gnawed her lip at the sight of empty desks, and began to imagine herself as a fading starlet watching the theater slowly empty.

"Have you seen those ships up close?" he said at dinner.

"No. I don't want to."

"They're shaped like giant cubes, with seven decks and round portholes along the sides. If I told you the price of a ticket it'd make your nose bleed."

"Why are they there? Why do they exist?"

"As a precaution—insurance for the rich. It's alarmism, if you ask me. The Machine will put this problem to bed soon enough."

"Right," she said, and stabbed a bowtie of pasta. "Right, right, right."

The dean called her into his office and told her things like "budget cuts" and "staff redundancy," while she dug a nail into a point on her scalp just behind her left ear, the way she'd done when she was a teenager who worried about how she looked in those jeans and what the other girls thought and what she could be if she couldn't be normal. On her way out, she carried her box of personal belongings past empty classrooms as blond hair fell from her head in single strands, in case she ever needed to find her way back.

■ ■ ■

In the morning, as he was leaving for the office, he noticed she was still slumped at the breakfast table in her pajamas, poking a congealed mass that had once been an egg on her plate.

"Aren't you going to work?" he asked.

When her tears started, he had enough sense to put his briefcase down. It took a pile of wadded tissues to dam the crying, after which he angled himself in the posture of a priest accepting confession, which in his mind was the most therapeutic arrangement.

"Personally, I'd love to not have to go to work. If I were in your shoes, I'd savor the opportunity to take some time off and collect my thoughts," he offered, attempting to sketch in a silver lining.

"You don't understand," she said. "I'm *useful*. I can't just be discarded. I'm like . . . I'm like the Machine. I have a purpose."

"I know. You'll be up and running again in no time," he said, but his arm around her shoulders felt like a prom night promise, the cheapest consolation prize.

She spent her days alone, watching the cumulonimbus churn and swallow the hours until nightfall. The patch in her hair grew wider, forcing her to comb in inventive ways to keep it concealed. She started smoking in the house, sucking down long thin French cigarettes, and retreated deeper into her books, letting the Bovaries and Kareninas plant flags in her lonely terrain.

Had he been a better reader, he would have known what was coming next.

He was sick again for the second time that month, only now he had a temperature and knew he couldn't work through it. He decided to leave the office early. They didn't really need the money anymore—the landlord hadn't been seen in three months and there wasn't much left to buy in stores. On his way up to the apartment, he passed by a man descending from their landing, though he didn't catch a good look. Apart from a pair of wire-rim glasses the stranger's face was swallowed in a fever haze.

He found her lying naked beneath the covers, a lit cigarette dangling off the edge of the nightstand. They stared at each other for a long terrible moment. She began speaking but he didn't try to understand the words. Instead he moved through the apartment breaking things in a calm and methodical way, seeing the hidden symbols and patterns of their time together and knowing that he had to dismantle them. In his mind, it was she who was doing the breaking.

■ ■ ■

Being at home with her felt like two people standing in a room trying to ignore the pile of skulls in the corner, and so he spent his nights in bars mustering the courage to sleep with another woman. Liquor offered the quickest escape from the rain and rising waters, so there was never a shortage of people with which to try his luck. But when he came to the crucial moment, the point when hair was curled around a finger and a head drew close and he could see the languid rise and fall of eyelashes, he thought again of the many small adulteries they would wage against each other, of the stale, stinking air they would let in once the door was opened, and he drew back into himself.

Finally he returned home one night and switched on all the lights and told her that if she wasn't planning to leave and he wasn't planning to leave then they had to agree there would be no escalation—that Mr. Wire-Rim Glasses was an aberrant leak and they would seal it for good.

She let out a breath and walked across the room and hugged him as if donning a life vest.

■ ■ ■

The day the Machine failed was warm and spring-like and they spent the morning imagining the many flowers that would bloom once the skies were clear. She wanted to stay home but he insisted they see the ceremony for themselves. They waded through ten blocks of dirty green water that came up to their thighs until a motor raft picked them up.

The crowd was so immense they could only get within a half-mile of the Machine, but still the sight filled them with awe, as if a god greater than the one clapping the deluge overhead had divined this mighty apparatus into being. The government had named it TEBA, perhaps hoping that packing so many syllables into a short acronym would be viewed as effective leadership. It was taller than any skyscraper, with two arcing structures curved around a thin central pillar—a steel and chrome claw threatening the heavens.

He tried to explain to her how it would work, lecturing about cadmium laser discharge and polyacrylic acid delivery systems and deionization thresholds. His voice rose to a childish pitch.

"It doesn't matter," she interrupted.

"Of course it does. These are the principles that are going to save the world."

"This," she said, indicating the sea of people staring wide-eyed at the Machine, as if their desperate faith could power it. "This is what matters."

He made a noise in his throat, the way he'd done when she told him about her visits to a psychic.

A voice emerged from the loudspeakers on the covered platform at the base of the Machine. A government official made a rambling speech about mankind's boundless ingenuity and indomitable spirit, and the crowd endured it in silence, careful not to offend the Machine with any lapse in courtesy.

At last, the crew activated TEBA. A great rumble rippled the water in every direction. A series of ascending lights rose up the central pillar until they reached the aperture at the top and a blue beam lanced into the sky. The clouds massed at the point of contact began to dissipate, and for a second the sun emerged. Then the beam cut off and the gray became total once more.

The Machine didn't explode, nor did it backfire and make the rains worse. It simply sputtered and stopped and, despite hours of attention from scientists and engineers, would not return to life. Finally, the official got on the microphone again and issued apologies before instructing the audience to disperse.

They were lucky to be on the edge of the crowd. He stood with his hands on his hips, wondering aloud how the technical problems could be resolved. She grabbed his arm and hurried him down a side street before the violence began in earnest.

■ ■ ■

The apartments in the floors below them were vacant, their neighbors forced out by the climbing water. The electric power flickered off, and so they lived by candlelight, pulling corks out with their teeth and letting the wine rush down their throats. They spent their afternoons beneath a tarp on the roof grilling burgers until there was no more coal, then they brought up rods and reels and cast into the water with their feet dangling off the roof's edge. The noise of the city faded a little more each night, until there was only the sound of water churning under the rain and they slept peacefully for the first time.

What died? The trees in the parks, the plants in the gardens, the animals in the zoo, the strays on the street, the homeless, the poor, the middle-class, the sick, the healthy, the dumb, the smart, the stores, the churches, the neighborhoods, and many, many children. What flourished? Mosquitoes, rats, carrion birds, people who took without remorse.

The good world was a graveyard, and there was so much mourning to be done they knew they'd never catch up, so they didn't make the attempt. Once a week they went scavenging for supplies, but otherwise they never left the apartment. They told each other jokes, secrets, painful stories, shedding the last layers that guarded their private selves until they stood before each other like exposed nerves. They made love without fuss or circumstance—an act as reflexive as yawning.

While fishing one day they saw one of the great ships pass by. The giant metal cube swam smoothly through the water, borne along by an enigmatic science. They heard the hum of its engines as it floated just a few feet away. The portholes were tinted black and they couldn't see inside, but they wondered if the passengers watched them with pity or envy. The ship clipped a building on the corner, causing the entire brick façade to crumble, but kept moving without pause, heading onward to an unknown destination, or perhaps merely to circle the world again and again until it once more resembled what the passengers wanted to see.

She pointed down at the destroyed building. "That used to be our laundry place," she said.

"Washing clothes seems a bit redundant nowadays."

"They did dry cleaning, too."

After they exhausted the local places, they had to go farther afield for supplies, and each time returned with less. She opened all the cabinets and counted their cans of fruit and bags of rice and bottles of water.

"What happens when we run out?" she asked. "Who's going to eat who?"

"Whom," he said.

"What?"

"Who will eat whom."

She smiled. "You really think grammar will be the last thing to go?"

"Once the food is gone, we'll have to fill our mouths with words."

■ ■ ■

A rustling sound in the kitchen woke them up one night. He put his hand on her shoulder, reached down for the baseball bat beside the bed, and told her to lock the door behind him. He lit a candle in the hallway and waited.

A man stepped into the light. The stranger was tall and hollow-cheeked, and though still young he had a dirty beard and chapped lips.

The man put his palms out slowly. "Just hungry," he said. "Not looking for trouble."

"This isn't the right place."

"Please," the stranger said. "A little kindness. I don't mean to hurt anyone."

"You need to leave right now."

The mask of supplication fell from the man's face.

He tightened his grip on the bat and a kind of intimacy took hold as they both realized what would come next. The man stepped forward, the candle flickered out, and in the darkness an ugly thing happened.

Afterward, she made him get into the tub and washed his cuts and bruises. She asked him what had happened to the stranger. He rubbed his eyes until they were rivered red and then told her.

He wanted to stay in the tub awhile so she left him alone. There were many things he thought he'd known about mankind, about the right way to live and the axioms born of high contemplation, but none of them had entered his mind when he did it. He'd felt only a soulless relief when the bat met flesh and bone. His skin damp against the tub's porcelain, he released his philosophies like a rich man gone poor.

■ ■ ■

The water seeped into the apartment and rose a few inches each day. At first they tried to bail with a pair of buckets, but they knew it was a futile gesture, and so they chased their vitamin D tablets with the remainder of the wine and resolved to send their little dingy under the waves in grand fashion. They took a can of paint from the back of the closet and marked their names across the walls in red swooping lines. They packed their photos, love letters, and a teardrop amulet from their third anniversary into a waterproof canister that they chained to the radiator so that it would mark this place as once having been more than a tomb.

On the last day, she waded into the bedroom in a white terrycloth robe covered in orange flowers and let it fall from her shoulders. He saw her ribs and hip bones jutting sharply against her skin as if attempting an escape, and his breath caught with sadness. She stared back at his nakedness. He'd been made ganglier from the months of want, a twig stripped of leaves. Still they managed to muster the old energy, at least as reminiscence, and he kissed her thin lips until they were bee-stung swollen. She climbed atop him and once more they were locked together, hands clawing for purchase on the sharp angles of their bodies, while in the distance tentacles of lightning probed down into the dead city.

■ ■ ■

That evening, part of the floor collapsed under the weight of the water, and they scrambled to grab their bags before running up to the roof. When the rain tore away the tarp, they were left exposed. They lay down on their backs beside each other, closed their eyes, and gripped hands.

"Will you miss me?" she asked.

"Of course not," he said. "You're not going anywhere."

The night surrendered to a gray morning as they lay shivering against each other, until the shivering finally stopped.

Another of the mighty cubes passed serenely through the water, rain sloughing off its sheer, perfect sides.

And though we had our faces pressed against the portholes, we did not want to see the two lovers with their hands still clasped, did not want to separate their story from the general run of sorrow, did not want to imagine what had been.

MARK CASSIDY

Juju

AFTER SEX MISS JOSEPHINE CLEANS HERSELF with water from the rain barrel on her stoop. She fills a silver bowl, normally used for washing her hands when she eats garri, and kneels astride it to scoop the water into the folds of her genitals with a cupped hand, raising each knee in turn while she balances her weight with the other hand, knuckles pressed into the floor. Outside her room the afternoon rain brings thunder and early darkness over the tin roofs of the houses round the yard.

Tell me something, I say.

Tell you what?

Anything.

She sighs, bends forward so that her braids fall from her shoulders and over her face, and says, Ok. Listen:

Two young girls, students from Uniport, travel to a small town in a neighboring state for a weekend break. They stay in a hotel. Could be a bush hotel or could be a fine town place with air conditioners in the rooms, maybe even CNN on the television. Doesn't matter. They toss their bags on the bed, wash, put on a little make-up and go out on the town to enjoy themselves.

First place they stop into, maybe someplace recommended to them by friends back home, they meet two men who say that they are from the capital, in town on business. Would the girls care to join them for some dinner and then some dancing? The two friends confer and agree that, as far as can be ascertained, these men are what they say they are and looking for nothing more than some fun away from their families, their wives in particular.

Of course, after the dancing, the girls go with the men to their rooms for sex and that's okay too. It's expected. Afterward they all dress and reconvene in one of the rooms to talk, to gossip, get to know one another a little better, continue drinking the Guinness and the Red Label whisky, the Five Alive juice, which the men have provided. During the conversation one of the men lifts an old-fashioned, battered suitcase onto the bed and opens it. It is full of money. Local currency but still, the girls are impressed. They glance at one another, eyes a little glittery with greed and drink, and ask what's going on. The man hands a wad of bills to each girl and invites them to lunch the following day. After that, the men say, they must travel on to the next place to continue with their business.

Josephine ties her braids up in a plastic shopping bag, wraps a towel round under her arms and steps outside in flip-flops to the communal shower. When she returns she sheds the towel and stands in front of the long, narrow mirror which leans against the wall beside the door, to apply her lotions, the Topifram and Skin Success, the Black Orchid, upon which she relies to care for and lighten her skin. A serious undertaking this, perhaps the most important activity of her day after her prayers. She carefully taps measured dollops from each pot into both palms and stirs them together with a fingertip before applying dabs all the way up her legs from her ankles onto her stomach, her breasts and over her shoulders, twisting to reach round to her back and her buttocks and finishing at her neck and throat. Rubbing follows application, again starting at her ankles and the tops of her feet, but this time moving more slowly and thoroughly in strokes and looping circles up along and around her entire body.

The following morning only one of the men appears at the agreed time. He explains that his friend is not feeling well, or maybe has unexpected business to attend to. The girl then without a partner, and again after discussing the situation with her friend, withdraws and returns to wait at the motel. The remaining couple eat their lunch—maybe it's okra soup, or egussi soup with garri—and then retire to the man's room for a last bout of lovemaking before he takes his leave. Again, afterward, he lifts the suitcase onto the bed and opens it, but this time empties all the money onto the sheets.

"What's this?" asks the girl.

"For you," says the man.

At that point, a knock comes at the door and his partner enters carrying not one but two more suitcases. The girl becomes nervous. The second man sets one bag on the floor, opens the other and dumps the contents, more money, onto the pile already there. Now she is frightened and starts to collect her clothes. The men tell her to relax, that nothing bad is going to happen, that all they want from her is a small favor, something which they believe she can provide and her friend cannot. They tell her that they want to make love to her together, a threesome, and that, if she agrees to this, they will seal the deal with a drink of whisky, or whatever she would like, and then get to the business.

She does not want to do it but greed gets the better of sense and she says yes. She starts to dress in preparation for going downstairs to the bar in the lobby for the drink. She believes that it might be necessary to have several drinks inside her before she can go through with what they want. She thinks that these might be rough men after all, that they might even want to do unusual things with her, but she is seeing a lot of money, a lifetime of money and comfort for her mum and her younger ones back in the village.

"Good," the man she was originally with says. "But let's not go downstairs for a drink. Not that we don't trust you but what if you change your mind and run away? We might not get another chance like this and, after the next town, we will be going back to our families and our opportunity will have passed."

"Plus," the other one says, winking and loosening his tie, "We'd like to sit with you, naked, and have the drink. That way we can get to the fun part without interruption, when we're ready."

Of course, after the first few sips of whisky the girl passes out. When she wakes the men and their luggage have gone. The money and her clothes remain. She remembers, as her head clears and she starts to pull on her things, that she has dreamed while she slept. She has dreamed that the men opened the third suitcase and removed a large snake, leaned over her where she lay on the bed, swaddled in cash, and opened her legs to introduce the head of the snake, its tongue flicking, eyes black as death, into her sex. She remembers that the serpent's long slick body disappeared completely inside her and then re-emerged, head first, to slither back into the bag. When she has finished dressing she looks for something in which to stash the money and goes to find her friend, to tell her what has happened.

When she's finished with the creams, having worked the last traces from her fingernails and the creases in her palms, Josephine leans and calls through the bars of the protector for one of the children in the yard to come, now that the rain has passed, so that she can give money to fetch mineral and soup.

The two friends return to the residence in the college and, the following day, the girl who went with the men starts to weep and finds that she cannot stop weeping. Fearful nightmares disrupt her sleep. The next day she falls sick and on the third day after her return to the city she dies.

I go chop. You want chop?

I stand up to dress. Sure. Suya. And beer. Not the happiest of endings.

In another version of the story the men with the snake attempt to trap both girls but one runs away and leaves her friend to suffer her tragic fate alone in the hotel room.

She reaches for the towel.

In a yet further rendition the girl who receives the serpent survives and goes on to establish herself in the town as a revered and wealthy Auntie, supplier of catering equipment and advice to the lonely, purveyor of juju charms upon request.

MARK CASSIDY

Man with Razor

LISTEN. HE KNEELS AT THE FOOT of the bed between her slender brown thighs, razor in one hand, dollop of foam dribbling from the fingers of the other, and clears his throat. I want to tell you something. She watches him, watches the razor and shakes her head, braids fanning, the multi-coloured beads at their tips clicking. Tiny muscles, like frets of chill wind on water, feather across her belly. Behind him the television mumbles. He shifts, leaning this way and that on his haunches, to smear the foam. She pulls back sharply, crumpling and bunching the bed sheets beneath her buttocks.

Relax. It's ok. I've done it a thousand times. So. Here's how it goes: A man, a famous singer, walks onto a stage and sits, rather leans, onto a high stool, one foot still on the floor, the other on a rung, like a lounge singer, like he might be Tony Bennett. He's wearing a black suit and white shirt open at the throat. Polished black shoes. He looks sharp. He looks glossy. His perfectly groomed hair catches the light from the overhead lamps. Beside him is a Spanish style guitar, such as a gypsy might use, resting upright on a chrome, rubber tipped stand. In front of him is another stand supporting two microphones, one set at sound hole level, the other positioned higher up, to receive his voice. That voice. The audience, quieted now, is waiting but he says nothing, sings nothing, does not reach for the guitar, reaches instead, without taking his eyes from the crowd, into a pocket of the suit jacket and takes something out. We, his disciples down in the dank well of the theatre, our hearts thumping in anticipation, might be thinking, Aha! A piece of paper. Something new! Lines, freshly blackened pages, from a work in progress. A bulletin from the front, which he is going to offer to us, run past us as it were, for our consideration. My friends, compadres, listen and tell me what you think. Or maybe it's a Jew's harp. Whatever it is, as he pulls his hand back into the open, into the light, it is something too small to see from even the first rows. He lifts his hand and draws it without hesitation, in a single, smooth stroke, down one side of his face, from the point of the cheekbone to the point of his chin, and then repeats the motion on the other side. He then rests his hand on his knee. Something in his fingers glitters. The audience, we beggars in the market, catches its collective breath. Only when he smiles, not a smile so much as a wide, forced grin, does the blood begin to flow. First, two lines which resemble fronts on a weather map appear, and then rivulets, following the creases in the skin, flow down over his neck and into his collar. Droplets fall onto his lapels, onto the front of his shirt, into his lap. He pushes the grin wider, ears lifting, eyes narrowing, and the flow of blood intensifies, soaking the front of his shirt, dripping down onto the boards at his feet. After a moment he returns the blade to the pocket, steps clear of the stool and walks past the guitar and off the stage.

He gets up from the floor and goes into the bathroom, returns with a glass of water which he dribbles slowly over the freshly denuded folds and clefts of her sex. He stoops to pat everything gently dry with a hand towel. I have talc.

Bring. Afterward she slots the little blue shaker into her purse.

You believe that? I heard that story when I was in school, way back, way out there on the flats of east central Alberta, and I believed it. It mattered. Then at least. The wind blowing all the time. Distance, anywhere I looked, slinking behind grain elevators, loping out beyond the last straggle of houses along the highway. Not true, obviously. There'd be scars. But, whatever I thought that was, I wanted it.

She tuts and raises her narrow hips from the bed. My friend, take. Such nonsense.

HEATHER BARTLETT

How to Choose

DON'T DO IT ALL AT ONCE. Break it apart. Break it down. Make smaller choices. One small choice: Yes or No.

"Are you lonely, Sweetheart?" No.

Push the button firmly so you can feel the click reverberate from fingertip to knuckle. While the system switches to the next recording, prepare yourself for the next choice. Straighten your spine and close your mouth. Close that mouth before you swallow dust, your mother used to say when she caught you lost in a book or memorizing numbers, your bottom jaw dangling from your cheeks.

Click your tongue to echo the start of a new recording.

"I've always wanted to walk across the Brooklyn Bridge." She sounds like the taffeta skirt that Sally, the receptionist, wears on Mixer Mondays. No.

Click. "I was married before. My daughter says it's time for me to date again. She says dads are supposed to want to know other people. I said I know enough, but here I am anyway. My wife died on a Sunday." He sounds like a corduroy blazer with worn elbow patches. Maybe they're iron-on patches. Maybe his wife used to do the ironing. Maybe she used to hang the blazer over her shoulders to feel its weight. Like Ex used to wear your socks and slide across the kitchen floor. Better than walking in your shoes, she would say.

Click.

The metal of the desk is oddly warm, but the back of the folding chair is cold, even through your sweater. In the middle of the desktop, the small buttons blink unevenly: blue for SAVE, red for NO. Someone has carved a heart under the blue button. The sharp etchings look more like scissors than a heart. The word *love* is carved in the back right corner, which someone has crossed out and written *divorce* underneath.

Lean forward, press your palms against the metal and arch your back like you're leaning in for a kiss. Go ahead and offer your lips to the air. Maybe this is how the person before you chose.

Sit back again. Let the cool spread up your back and into your neck like goosebumps. Adjust your headset and turn up the volume. Close your eyes this time.

"What they don't tell you is that once you speak into this recorder, your voice isn't yours anymore." When you were eleven, you always sat next to Alice on the bus. You both lived toward the end of the long bus route. You both preferred listening to speaking. "It's out there with you, whoever you are, in some generic room, where you're supposed to decide if you want to fuck me based on my words." You pulled your knees to your chests and your jackets over your heads. It doesn't matter if it was you or if it was Alice, and you can't really remember, but one of you started talking. Alice wanted to know what it must be like to be caressed. You wanted to know what it must be like to touch. "What do you hear? A woman you want to choose? Or are you already reaching for the red button?" When the bus turned onto Third Street, you pulled the jackets down and laughed as you passed the corner market, even though you were never sure what was funny.

Push the button. You said you'd listen to five today.

■ ■ ■

It's been raining since you woke up, heavy, steady rain, the kind that makes you feel clean even before you shower. You'd planned to come tomorrow, but you like the sound of water dripping off your shoes onto the hard floor while you choose. Today is better.

Sally takes your umbrella and hands you the plastic In Use door tag. She offers you a cupcake left over from last night's mixer. "I really wish you'd join us." She tells you this every week. "Don't you want to put faces to those voices?"

You're in room twenty-three again today. The rain from your shoes leaks across the linoleum, trickling toward the back corner. Feel how wet your hair is when you put on the headset. Press the dampness into your scalp when you adjust it. My wet-headed stepchild, Ex used to call you. Wet hair has always calmed you. Your level of anxiety could be measured by the frequency of your showers. There were times that you showered three times a day just to keep from arguing. You can't rinse it away, Ex would say. But you tried.

Someone has outlined the scissor-heart in permanent marker.

■ ■ ■

Let the connection begin with words. The commercial doesn't show any images, just the text on the screen. Faint flute melody accompanies a voiceover that reminds you of the self help radio shows your mom listened to in the mornings: How to Be Your Best Self, How to Make Him Notice You, How to Choose You. She listened while making breakfast. I'm okay, you're okay, she would repeat to herself and pat your head.

It's time to choose Moore, Inc. The text fades into the dark blue screen.

Everyone is always talking about time. Time to date. Time to move on. Time to try again. Time for more.

"But it's only 3:30." Even when it's not 3:30, this always feels like the appropriate response. On those first nights, when neither of you wanted to give in to sleep, Ex would nudge you—push her palm against your neck, bend her knee against your back, knead a toe into your calf. You would nudge back and ask what time it was. All night, it was 3:30.

■ ■ ■

The room always feels the same: empty. This is the point. To make you want to fill the space with words. With voices. With choices.

Use the space differently today. Sit on the desk and lean your back against the bare wall. Put your feet on the chair. Take your shoes off. When you were a kid, you always took your shoes off so your footprints wouldn't give you away. In third grade, you didn't want your mother to know that you let Billy kiss you on the playground when his friends weren't looking. A pebble from your shoe might have given it away. In fourth grade, you didn't want her to know that you didn't go to the playground anymore.

From this angle, the scissor-heart looks like a raised eyebrow to the blinking button-eyes.

"How many of us will admit that we are here because we failed at doing it the right way?" He sounds like the college professor whose class you used to skip because it was at the same time as your roommate's free period. The two of you would smoke pot in the bathroom and sometimes fuck in one of your twin beds before going to your British Authors survey class. Click.

"Maybe right now, I'm in the next room listening to *your* words." Knock softly against the wall. No response.

When your feet get cold, it's time to leave. Ex still has your favorite pair of wool socks. Remember to tell Sally you will not be attending the Mixer.

■ ■ ■

Moore, Inc. is hard to find if you don't know what you're looking for. The building sits back from the street, shielded by a row of overgrown shrubs. Look for mailbox #1985. The white letters are worn away; one of the 'O's is completely gone, leaving a faded 'MO RE' on the blue mailbox to assure singles they're in the right place. Follow the cement walkway.

The facility isn't much to look at when you walk up to it. The two-story brick building is neither impressive nor intimidating. The blue awning barely provides any shade. Maybe that's the point.

The door is glass. There is no buzzer. Walk in.

A dark haired woman is watching you from her desk across the room. She and the desk are the only things in the large, open lobby. She stands up and fluffs her hair, tucks a thumb into her back pocket. She trips a little when the heel of her red pump slides across the tile floor, but she catches herself. Pretend not to notice.

"Congratulations on choosing Moore." You're surprised her voice doesn't echo off the hard walls. She hands you a clipboard and click pen. "I'm Sally." She pats the edge of her desk as she walks back around to sit. "Just need some basic information to get you started."

While you scribble your phone number and mailing address, Sally pulls a pack of silver disks from her desk drawer. While you check off boxes under *Interested in* and *Interested in Hearing From,* she taps a fingernail against the plastic cases. Click the pen and fasten it to the clipboard. Done.

As she leads you down the hallway, she hands you a blank disc and an instruction card. The laminate feels oily in your hand.

Don't: Give your name or any personal details.

Do: Share your relationship philosophy with a potential mate.

Sally recognizes your open mouth as hesitation. "Just start with some words about what you're looking for," she says. Close your mouth.

Sally accidentally leaves the plastic *Recording* tag on the inside door-knob. Leave it. Take stock of the room now that you're finally alone: clean walls, metal folding chair, metal desk, blue and red buttons, recorder and microphone. Insert the blank disc. Push *Record.* Start talking.

■ ■ ■

"I don't believe in matchmaking. I don't believe in this system. But I've come to accept that I need to try to work within it." This one sounds young. Like a grad student who doesn't have time to go out and find dates, but wants something. Something. This one sounds like you. When you were young and always nodded in recognition when someone quoted Aristotle's Poetics, even though you didn't know. When you wanted to know.

Click. The button is sticky today. Push it again to release it.

You push all *my* buttons, Ex would say while unbuttoning your shirt, now it's my turn. It often started this way. So you wanted to talk about why she never called you back? Pushing buttons. You wanted to know who taped the note to the door? Pushing buttons. You wanted more? Pushing. Sometimes you didn't mind, though. Sometimes you pushed just to get pushed back.

How many are you going to hear today? Tomorrow it might rain.

■ ■ ■

Today you're going to listen to follow-up tapes from your SAVED list. "The rules are the same for follow-ups." Sally is smiling and touching your arm. "If you still choose to save them, push the blue button."

You can't save me, Ex would say.

Thank Sally and close the door. Adjust your headset. Turn the volume down until you can't make out what's being said, then turn it up one notch. There are three to hear today.

One: "If you saved me, you must have heard something you like." Remember his voice. You do like it. He sounds like the guitar riffs your neighbor plays before bed. "Now you're listening again for something more." You're going to want more, Ex would say, closing the door behind her. Click.

Two: "The instructions say not to reveal too much in these recordings." He still sounds sad. This is what you like about him.

You thought Ex didn't know about the cigarettes you kept under the empty flower pot. You would sit on the cement steps and smoke after she'd gone home. When confronted, you thought about lying, saying they were left from before you quit, you didn't even know they were there. You thought about blaming someone else, the neighbor who plays the guitar. But you didn't. You nodded. She didn't bring it up again.

Click.

Three: This one starts with silence. This is what you remember. This is why you like her. She inhales sharply before speaking. "Yesterday I hiked to the top of the gorge. It took all morning, and when I got to the top, my heart was beating so loudly I couldn't see." You don't see me, one of you would say. It didn't matter if it was you or if it was Ex; one of you would always say it. "I started counting loose rocks until the waterfall came back into focus." But no matter who said it, you were always first to apologize. "It looked smaller than it had from the bottom."

■ ■ ■

Do: speak naturally and clearly.

Don't: hold the microphone too close to your mouth.

Say something about looking for more.

No. Say you're not looking for more.

Don't hold the microphone so close to your mouth. Delete and start again.

■ ■ ■

Sally offers you a cupcake with extra sprinkles. The sprinkles are blue. The extras are in a clear plastic cup. She shakes them. "Maybe if you just came once." That's right; today is Tuesday. She has a sprinkle stuck to her shirt collar. Don't tell her. "Maybe it's better to look in a person's eyes."

Maybe it's better this way, Ex said.

You were re-packing the box your mother had sent you. From the very start, you just never wanted to keep your shoes on, her note said. You wrapped the tiny sneakers in tissue paper and put them in last, on top of the purple blanket your mother had been knitting since before you even told her. The just-in-case-blanket. That's what your mother called it. That's why I chose purple, she said, it works either way. You taped up the box and carefully printed the return label with permanent maker.

It's better this way, Ex said and wrapped her arms around herself. We didn't have a choice, she said.

You shook the box as you picked it up.

■ ■ ■

Run your fingers over the scissor-heart. Feel the uneven edges of the etching. When you were thirteen, you started etching words into your skin. Rub your forearm where it once said *yes,* your inner thigh where it said *and.*

Put the headphones down. Let the recording play out without listening. Instead, search your pocket for something sharp enough to write with—a paperclip. Unfold it and scrape against the desk surface. It sounds like chalk. Press harder. Carefully carve a word into the metal. Keep the letters small and precise—*c h o o s e.*

Cross it out.

■ ■ ■

Do: remain anonymous.

Don't: forget to be yourself.

■ ■ ■

I don't know you. That was the first thing you said.

You make me nervous. That was the second.

Ex pulled her chair closer to yours. So close that your knees were touching. She probably asked what you wanted to know, but you couldn't hear her. Your knees were touching. It was a Sunday.

On Sundays you drank mimosas and fucked in the shower. You ate whatever was leftover from the refrigerator, broken up into bite-sized pieces. Ex took smaller bites than you did.

You spread the newspaper across the bed and took turns reading the editorials. Sometimes you would read headlines out loud and use them to invent stories. SHOCK WAVE HITS COMMUNITY: You gave a slow account of tidal waves hitting the sustainable sand community you built at the beach with a curly haired child. Ex crafted a conspiracy about power lines and a shadow government.

When it got dark, she would hold out closed fists and say, Choose. One fist held the car key, the other was empty. If you chose the empty fist, she would take you by the wrist and lead you back to bed; sometimes she would spend the night. If you chose the car key, you spent the night alone.

On the last Sunday you bought champagne. This wasn't supposed to be the last Sunday; it was supposed to have been the Sunday before, but on Friday you asked for another, just one more to say all the words you both needed to say. What words, Ex wanted to know. You wanted to know, too, you did. But really, you just wanted more.

The car was full with her life: repurposed wine boxes—Pinot Noir crossed out and replaced with KITCHEN in black marker, queen sized blankets in plastic garbage bags, clothes in stacked piles on the back seat, a shoe box of homemade mixed CDs on the front passenger seat. Only one box of books, you noticed. All anyone needs are the beat poets, anyway, she said.

You decided not to open the champagne. Take it, you said, and anchored the bottle between two stacks of jeans.

You make me nervous. That was the last thing she said.

You don't know me. That was the last thing you said.

ZACH WEBER

The World's Sixteen Crucified Saviors

N EVER HAVE I SOMETIMES ALWAYS EXISTED.

■ ■ ■

I see him and think: won't it be lovely? Stand around and chat. Five minutes later I am caught in a conversation, disappointing both him and myself. Nothing worse. So I'll sit here under the tree by the stone building, by the bookstore, under the tree with the long branches and the light sprinkled like salt through them, reading my book. It needs reading and if I close it now, I'll never finish it.

I set down my book and rise to meet my friend. His name is Ktskh. This is important, what we're doing. I'll finish the book later. We shake hands. Other students pass us on their way to the bookstore. He asks if I'm going to Chaulat's party tonight. I am there, having a bad time, holding a beer. I tell him no, noticing as he walks away that someone has stolen my book and book bag. Another detail lost in the foam.

■ ■ ■

I purchase a book in the student bookstore. Selected Works of Andrey Kolmogorov. I tell the clerk that I am in Advanced Probability and Topology II. She doesn't care. A thousand times she cares. More often than not she doesn't and I frown and leave. I am walking home in the dark, having finished the Selected Works, and am accosted by a gentleman with a familiar voice. He beats me thoroughly and robs me of my belongings. I do not buy the book, though I consider it. Instead I purchase a collection of early Fantastic Four from the comic book section. I harbor a deep sympathetic relationship, albeit necessarily one sided, with Reid Richards, insofar as he was another man who knew what it was like to be in two places at once.

■ ■ ■

There, I motion towards Miranda with a limp hand, and she promptly increases the distance between our physical bodies. I am sixteen and I've just met a girl named Miranda. She asks me if I'd like to go out sometime. I tell her I'm dating Zhou-Dzi Li-Tzen from Staffordshire High. She shrugs and smiles and says that's okay. Next Friday I am at the movies with Miranda. The film is *Hot Treasure*. I am attending *Hot Treasure* with Zhou. I am there alone. I have known Miranda for five years now. I kissed her goodnight on that date. She has told me since that she wouldn't go on a second date with a guy who didn't go for a kiss on the first. She appreciates the confidence. I still watch *Hot Treasure* on television and I haven't seen it since then. The memory of it is painful and wonderful, loaded. We are sixteen and she is leaving the theater and I give her a hug and inquire as to whether she would be interested in a second date. She asks me to let her think about it. It will be fine.

■ ■ ■

I am alone. I am thirty, forty. I think often of Miranda and sometimes even Zhou, who I haven't seen in twelve, twenty-two years. Zhou and I are married and she asks me what I want for my thirty-fifth birthday. It is Zhou's twenty-first birthday and I am proposing to her. I knew we'd wed. I am with Miranda on the beach and I'm twenty-five on the eve of America's Decacentennial Celebration. I've just gestured towards her with my limp hand and she has just moved away, across the sand, across the fire. I am lighting the fire by pouring lighter fluid over charcoal and driftwood. I am squatting with the lit match, touching it to the oily patch that gleams at the edge of coals in the last minutes of the molten beach sunlight, a walk away from our ancestors who got stuck in the foam, whose hearts are salty green.

I have always never existed sometimes. In my brutal infancy I am tormented most by the impenetrable roaring void. From seventeen through fifty-two it is the fact that the world in which I am not burdened my peculiar omniscience is only a slim percentage of my experience. In my brief flashes of normal life I am shown what it would be like to sit at the edge of the sea of information, gaze upon it and wonder what might lie beneath, rather than to be submerged in it, constantly swimming up at a ray of light that is maybe just the absence of darkness. And I have never sometimes always existed too.

I am sixteen and fifty-two. At fifty-two I am accelerating towards the end. The last thirty-five years have always been leading to this, particularly since I am twenty-five and on the beach with Miranda and she says that I'll never see her again. At sixteen I'm standing under bristling storm clouds outside of the movie theater, waiting for Miranda. It is sunny and I am alone. At sixteen I am being born and am at the edge of the end. I am twenty-one and I can't stop crying. I've seen everyone I love die in every way imaginable. I've always seen it and it makes me sad. I cry in the car and at home and I curl fetal on the hardwood floor, dry-heaving under a cat's inquisitive gaze.

I am outracing myself to the edge of this universe, where it all begins again, just the same, closer than a mirror, a surface always curving, subtly, with the dynamic tension of two realities touching hips, where along the fault line one can glimpse the Nothing that could have been if no thing had ever been, a hairline crack between worlds impassable by any craft conceived by man, and I see myself and I nod and we are on the beaches at night, watching the foams recede, knees at our chests, fires burning, trying not to think.

■ ■ ■

At the CVS buying fucking Diet Coke and candy. Buying cigarettes. Three Heads appear before me in the void. Their spinal cords dangle like dead snakes from their precision-cut necks. Cerebrospinal fluid drips into a blackness that fades away into the condensation on my Diet Coke. The cashier bags my goods and bids me a friendly *ete re nous atxevo. Ete re nous* could be a cry for help but I don't give a shit about anyone else. I leave wondering how anyone's supposed to figure out how to live.

■ ■ ■

Different beach now. Dark still. Storm approaching. Here and there I'm alone but I know a woman named Miranda with whom I'm deeply in love. Sometimes she's there with me. I want to fuck her on the sand. I want to weep to shame the ocean. To make this storm seem anemic in comparison. I'd like to cry out until my voice breaks like a thunderclap and my chest burns like I've been struck by lightning, whatever my soul is, pulled upward, upward, my body discarded like a damp towel. I lie in the wet sand like a primordial specimen and listen to Corcovado playing faintly from a beach house down the row. The meaning of existence, my love.

I refuse to discuss the dream. Here it is. It isn't a dream. Four times it happened. Rows and rows of bare steel pylons extend, in all directions, for one hundred miles from the center of an empty city at night. The base of each pylon forms a sort of upside-down 'V' shape which measures, from ground to vertex, exactly four meters, and then from the vertex to the light at the top is no more nor any less than twelve meters. Atop each pylon sits a high pressure sodium lightbulb, shining against the hard night like a gem in the void, a hundred thousand lacerations in the fabric of the vault of heaven.

Weaving in between these structures are the spirits of the deceased from all around the world, each one carrying a quiet fire in their belly. I stand and watch them float along, in the bright light, returning home.

I see those ghosting teens I used to know, sitting on the curb in front of the Shop-N-Save between Sycamore Street and Mountainview Boulevard, catcalling to blistered corpses that swell and wheeze hot dry air from every hole in a grim semblance of life.

—Damn, you got a ass like a onion. Make me wanna cry.

—Come talk to me girl. Lend me some sugar. I am your neighbor.

—Nah, come over here. What were you like when you was alive?

—. . .

—Shit, I aint tryin to get into nothin serious. I just wanted to fuck you.

Life might be an infinite number of movies all being played at different speeds and with a constantly revolving audience. We all need a witness to our experience.

At twenty-four and twenty-seven I'm with Miranda in Kerala. I see a print of the goddess Kali by Raja Ravi Varma and it's uncomfortably arousing. When Miranda catches me staring at it, she thinks it's cause it's a painting with blue tits in it. I don't tell her that the man she is trampling beneath her feet is her husband, Shiva, who, in one interpretation of the legend, willingly puts himself in this position, choosing to submit to his wife in her most raw and powerful manifestation. Kali is a force of destruction in the form of time which is above time itself. I have stared into the heart of the Black One. I think she's sexy.

The words taste bad. When I'm not a character in a book I feel like I have more control but a lot of times I know that control is an illusion. Things happen because they do. It's not fate or God. It's less mystical than chance, even. What happens just happens. We think we have choices but our choices are just occurrences and so they happen just like a leaf falling happens. When I get to know that control is an illusion and I lay by Miranda maybe while we drift in orbit around some planet so far from Earth that you forget Earth exists, I maybe also touch her cheek while she sleeps and remember that she'll die.

■ ■ ■

I met Miranda at a college party that I didn't attend. She was majoring in Concentration. I could never quite grasp it. She told me about her ex-boyfriend, without naming him. I thought that it was a curious thing to discuss with a relative stranger but she was very beautiful so I let her continue. After awhile the man she was describing began to sound terribly familiar. I asked her if she wasn't actually talking about a young man with whom I'd attended high school. I asked her his name and she confirmed my suspicion. I said some things never change and we laughed over our drinks.

Poetry

CHELSEA DINGMAN

Wintersong

December's cold comes to pity us again,
fields stormed by dry riverbeds & dead leaves.
I'm afraid, but I don't want to tell you.
The baby hasn't moved & there is blood
where there shouldn't be. My body,
less godlike when still, cleaves to yours, almost

whole when someone else is inside. Almost
sane, I imagine our daughter again,
the vine-like cord wrapped around her body.
On the news, there is a woman who leaves
her child on a schoolroom floor, covered in blood,
& no one is safe. Not even us. You

know the truth: I've only ever loved you.
Even when we were power lines, almost
breaking under snow. There's blood
on my thighs & I call you home again,
but we've never been people to choose who leaves.
Tonight, each psalm we know is a body

broken off in our teeth, the baptism of a body
we will never touch back from blue, but you
sing anyway, hands clasped like leaves
around my swollen belly. Something is always almost
breaking inside me when you touch me. Again,
birth is sometimes about destruction: blood

& shit & sound. Or no sound. Just blood
we want to reinvent inside the body—
what happens if we break all the way open again?
Without the tiny bloom of her, will I be enough for you?
In this failure: hunger-songs like a firing squad. Almost
brave, I want to run for our lives, to leave

this cold ground beneath us, the leaves
like ghosts I can't give away. Like blood.
We were almost in love yesterday. Almost
sane. I turned you on, my body
swollen like sky you want to part. A promise you
will love me when you can't. Again,

we blossom & break, leaves in a gutter. Again,
blood when I bend. For a few months, you
were almost real. The lyric, longing a body.

SHERRAINE PATE WILLIAMS

Staying Alive

as I can and I don't care anything about Tony
Manero's new life in Manhattan. Fuck that rapist fuck.
No, he didn't do Annette, he only watched. But what stuck
with me was the hurt his silence approved. Maybe Joey
and Double J rode that train but I'm sure that Stephanie
could tell you a different story—that some girls' luck
has nothing to do with winning a dance contest, dumb schmuck
that she was for letting him in later, or ever. See,

this time and place has a way of saying he's okay,
that he's smooth with his slick moves, and it's only
such a heartthrob is trapped by his poor circumstances
so we'll still call him hero and root for his sweet day

in the limelight. But ask any Annette, or me, if she
feels like the cunt he calls her, after. She only wanted to dance.

JEHANNE DUBROW

Gadfly

After Robert Hass

Many days, for a few months last year,
my friend would call to ask if I
had taken my alprazolam, which stilled
the panicked wings inside my chest.
They were pills the size of larvae.
I broke them in half like tiny bodies
split, laid a piece on my tongue
and swallowed with my own spit.
Early afternoons. I paced from porch
to living room, traveling miles of floor.
My friend's voice on the phone was a net—
she caught me in my movements.
I hear her speaking now and remember
the nervous flying of my hands.
I must have sounded to her like a thing
that buzzes as it nears the dying
light above a door. I took the pills
or didn't—depending on how much
I'd closed my eyes the night before,
trapped in the clear bottle
of sleep and no way of getting out.
Difficult to describe my disquiet,
except to say my fingers hovered
between the slats of window blinds,

opening a small exit on the street.
I think of the ancient story—the girl
who fled desire lowing in a field,
knowing the gods transform us
out of love or loathing, foot become hoof
and the delicate brow given horns,
stung and stung by a fly, how she cried
for the red welts that mean living.
Hunched with the phone to my ear,
I bit a pill to powder. My friend talked
and listened, listened and talked.
And I, was I the weeping or the stinging,
Io or insect, pursuing myself through
the iridescent cruelty of that year.

CATHERINE PIERCE

In Which the Country Is an Abandoned Amusement Park

Here is the wrecked Zipper, its cages
warrened now with rabbits and crabgrass.
Here is the splintering concession stand.
Once you bought cotton candy and gave
not a thought to how something so very
there was instantly so very *not*, only the pinging
afterfeel of sugar against your molars.
Here is the wooden coaster. Once it hurtled
down the tracks and you threw your hands
high and shrieked. It was a lark then
to be helpless, to know your car
might careen off the curve and launch
into the far-below pines, but probably not.
Here is a funhouse. How was it fun,
once, to see your face as not your face?
You try to remember, but your mouth
is so warped, and your eyes look wider
with every step. Like you could fall into them.
Like they can't believe what they're seeing.

LEILA CHATTI

Nulligravida Nocturne

"And they ask you about menstruation. Say, 'It is harm, so keep away from
wives during menstruation. And do not approach them until they are pure.'"
—THE HOLY QUR'AN, 2:222

He touches me.
Reaches across our mattress

on the floor like a raft, adrift in night's black
gulf. Headlights glide over the opposite wall.

Gilded. Quick. His hands
cresting the waves of my hips.

In the dark, I leak
more darkness. Inside,

an endless well. I know
now, deep within myself, myself

as harmed. Know deeper
the man I love

will never harm me. He's no god
but good

to me. Like blood, the night
comes and comes and

comes. I was taught
for years a touch like this

was fruitless, a sin
to love when love couldn't

root as proof. His
hands on my hips despite,

moored. If asked,
I'd make the trade—give up the inconceivable

heaven for a warmth
I can sense, the faithless

man who draws me toward him
through shadow, knowing

who I am, what I can't be.

Stray

The lamb is bleating circles round the pasture.
He slipped from his enclosure like a soul—
through three fences!—and because he's still nursing,
his calls draw alarming response from the herd.

He won't come to me, though I want to help,
this one they call Freezer for his not-distant future,
this one of ginger wool the color and texture
of my dead grandfather's hair behind his Bible.

And lo, there will be joyful celebration
when the shepherd delivers the stray back to his flock,
the ewe's teats near to bursting at his return.

How nice the little handfuls of my own
mammal breasts have felt when I cup them,
buoyed up above their human flesh.

You think the space you occupy is large
and then—You think your one life precious—

MARGARET MACKINNON

John Baptizes Jesus at the Odney Pool

After a painting by the English artist Stanley Spencer (1891-1959)

You had not known you belonged to such a region
until Spencer took you there, until he showed you
Cookham, where God made a detour down High Street,

past Fernlea to the Odney Pool,
mineral-laced water near the Thames
where the artist once swam as a child.

All's inverted now. Heaven's here—
in the languid pool, where, amid the bathers
in their ordinary, black-knit suits, God's only Son's

made known. Here's John, an odd man in skins,
bristled and untamed, and Jesus, his face
that of any villager. No one seems surprised

as this little miracle unfurls. The scene is crowded,
narrow space filled with the press of bathers
on this afternoon of gossip, summer voices

left over from childhood's drowsing.
Some of the villagers are napping, stretched out
in quiet leisure on the bleached stone steps.

Others gaze calmly as John pours water
from a copper bowl over the head of God's
beloved boy. Why should they stand amazed?

It is you who are changed in this anointing,
seeing the world through the painter's eyes,
its cold waters turned tender and familiar

in the fading light, this low cast that alters all.
Remote things join in me, Spencer wrote.
Life quickens here—

Of course, they'll all depart too soon,
making their way back toward tidy houses,
predictable patterns, now rearranged—

but look, before you leave,
at the broad water-meadows that flood each spring,
where color's splashed

on this dully-lit summer day,
where you seek some last pleasure
in the pale English sun. And there—

you can just see those three lone trees
he painted, trees his young daughters loved
for the way they seem to march past

the horizon to some other world—
and always back to Cookham, its quiet lanes
where none of us is missing now.

Dear P.

If you are   like me and can   only see the horizon

that is unreachable   don't know that want   sheds and

grows and   sheds and   grows   please don't

keep trying   the outline   is fine find a closer

aisle pull the cans and boxes   from the shelves so

you can   eat   so you can feed on likeness   anything

is possible but   the possible isn't always   foldable

it's okay to not spin the   diamond   that begs for your

finger it's okay to   reach   behind you allow your clothes

to   snag onto   air to hide in   time   to exist in

the stars to believe that awards   signify   nothing it is

okay to only watch the birds in the   ficus tree clutter the

branches each season   leave   their waste and let

your hands be   hands   and the   wings be wings

SONIA GREENFIELD

Women & Children First

When the wind changes direction,
smoke shifts from the fires, so sometimes
it's burning tires in my face, other times
it's meat. Reader, I have done what I can
for you. Gave you my extra Sig
& taught you how to shoot; showed you
which mushrooms are safe to eat; even
trained you to avoid congregations
of carrion flies & the decay they make
love to. If food was plentiful, I shared it.
If the moon only shone on empty woods
or handfuls of bright sequins drummed up
by breeze across the lake, we laughed at
nothing in particular. Now, there's a menace,
a madman pulling off each fence board
at the rear of the yard & I'm crouching
with you, a few bullets left between us.
Reader, I have this child clinging to my leg,
his eyes crazed with fear, his sweaty face
flecked with dirt. The sounds of splintering
wood & hound-like baying make our hackles
rise. You look to me for help, but my field
of vision narrows, only able to take in
the one I would kill to save. I love you,
but you know how it must be. Grab your
gun, Reader. Run, Reader. Lakshmi Singh
says the hordes are on the move &
from this point on you're dead to me.

I Pump Milk like a Boss

I pump milk on the side of the road where the grass is biblical green
as if first cousin to the cow, her pink and swollen tits immaculate

as the plumbing of a church organ sending up calls to god, brassy mesh
of notes, fermented and dank as kush. I pump milk with my bare hands

into a bar's bathroom sink, above which is a mirror where someone's scrawled
I Love Cricket Pussy and below that, Everyone Deserves to be Loved.

I look at myself under the fingered smudge, the bodily fluids spattered
like haikus and I pump as if my milk is propaganda,

fingers bowing across my chest like a pawn shop violin,
milky graffiti tagging the spit-clogged drain.

I pump like I'm writing my name in blood
which turns to the milk my child sucks dry, which she turns into blood.

I pump like I have a tattoo on my pudenda
that says Aerosmith backwards, I pump

as if my hands have teeth, one combat boot hitched up on the toilet seat,
each hiss of milk chanting like a choir *yes bitch yes,*

my tits bitten and salt-veined, as when my baby
took her first gulp of air, humming

POETRY

103

from the engorged crevasse of me
like a herd of wildebeest, as if the hive of me could have burst,

the infrared honey, the *glop glop*
of afterbirth dripping down my left leg,

spittle and amen, amniotic residue
fluorescent with prayer—

Do men lactate is a popular Google search and I wonder
what would happen if they could, our presidents

lifting their offspring to their breasts in the deep pockets
of night, listening to the dribble of milk

sipped from the pulpit of their bodies. Tonight my breasts
became so engorged I said I'd pay someone to suck my tits

half-joking. But a woman who heard followed me to the bathroom, read me

a sex poem while I pumped my milk, leaning away from the need in her voice

and the milk came slow and I pumped and waited for her to finish
and a street light scribbled in the parking lot

and I know there is a price we pay for loneliness
and a price we pay to forget it and I dedicate my libido

to my younger self and this is how I want to live, milk-stained, a little bit emptied,
a little bit in love with the abundance of my body,

my milk pale yellow with a layer of cream
which I will save long after it's turned, praising its curdled glow

every time I open the fridge, as if its presence is enough to keep me safe,
as if it's enough to make me invincible.

GINA FRANCO

Throne

After James Hampton's The Throne of the Third Heaven of the Nations
Millennium General Assembly

"Where There Is No Vision The People Perish"—**HAMPTON**, Proverbs 29:18

To happen on it, resplendent in its vault. Body of
    echoes, body of borrowed light. As if sealed,
a book has been opened; indecipherable, now
    the script glances with imminent signs (—*but who*
can see it to completion—?) Foil over foil and still luster
    only darkens
                the face of the deep. And only
later is this everywhere familiar. The bay nearing
    low tide. Midday sun. The whole shore a flattened
mirror, and as far as we could see the world was all
    light on water, our walking rippling
through many surfaces—sky/sea, sand/clouds—
    our stepping into reflections and leaving
                    invisible
impressions in the path . . . image of aisle and horizon,
    as though a destination has laid itself down,
at last, before time . . . image of the sea spewing up
    its dead, as though something endless is about
to begin . . . with meaning
                nearing, but ever nearing
beyond reach, like a really good dream. So the deep
    will have its monsters. So flesh beyond recognition. What a man
will do to another man. To his God. What a man
    will see, left alone. With his book.

There is vision and there is
        the threat of emptiness in vision . . . image of
the bare throne beneath its glinting tin: waste, ruin, garbage:
        the moon hanging over the dirty beach,
the moon gathering dust around it, glowing its dead gold glow

■ ■ ■

        into the vault of the sky. Into the everything,
largely, to be given up, refused, before being
        can return to its king. Into what-is, ever
shrouded within what-ought-to-be. What was,
        in the old allegories, the end of all
                                        thrones: home
coming. Into the waking
                                to thin snow on the frozen again
garden beds after a false spring tricked the lamb's
ear back before time. Moonflower, crowning tulip
        bulbs, fools
                        of a certain soullessness. It is bitter
cold, and we knew that man in the empty lot had
        no place to sleep. That he stepped from the shadows
a shadow—least of these—and blessed us as we
        idled past, turned away, looked ahead
                                        to the exit
        that leads to the road going home.
                                Easy. To be

touched from this distance now as if light
will flicker in darkness, and darkness
        will fail to recognize it. To admit
to cruelty that belongs, after long alleviation
        of time and remove, to another
you. The one made up
                                    of incandescent idols
of soul. The one that thinks beauty
        is enough and resents that there is not
enough of it. Sun. Water in a clear glass
        pitcher on the breakfast table. Corona
of light breaking over the scarred dark
        wood. Like the sculpture gleaming away
its vault, the sculpture overshadowing
        the otherwise emptied lot—perfect
                        elegy—
in which the worst you've done is bettered,
        and you are consoled in the event
of grieving. For
                            there is always grieving. Always
        the cathedral mind longs to be
                                    the fire
in the bulb, not the bulb. The lord, not the lord's
        throne. And this is the beginning
of becoming
        meaner, where little is freely given
up, in case it proves itself

■ ■ ■

needful. After all. Because
what if the mind is
a hovel, finally, and the kingdom
being built there is paper and tinsel in a dark
room. Room over room, so hidden
it doesn't exist. In the streetlamp
raining in
the window, there's a passerby
(caught fleetingly)
in spotlight. Then a small shed, besides. Little
outside to notice, to tell what may lie
inside,
advancing. Little sign. Not even gravity
in the look of things, such is the silence
of such poverty. Lightless, the tiresome
sameness of the downpour, its sad
angle. Too bad the category for what is lacking
in things is apathy. Too bad the category
for darkness is
reigning
all in its wake. What it will erase
to see itself being seen
(, there,)
among the white garments in the kingdom
of the mind. Invisible builder, invisible visitor
apparitions. Nonetheless speaking into the hollow. Repeating
themselves in symmetrical dreams
(—*fear*
not—)
(—*do not be*
afraid—) and forms. Because what if to be
a sign is to be

■ ■ ■

something else also. A promise?
A deferment. In which what matters seems
　　(not yet?)
evident. A betrothal. In which what is
　　present is
　　　　　　　(at the crux)
absent. Someone saying you complain
　　though it's not yet finished. Wait for it
to be done. But what *is*
　　to be done? Night garden, star
　　-light. Moon
again, orange, huge
　　　　　　　as it should
　　be, hanging
over the horse farm one of the nights I waited for
　　you to come home. Wind, clouds
racing through the sky. The field made grave as the moon, now
　　overcast, is snuffed out,
　　　suddenly. Hope. Holding
out for an end of waiting, as
　　if a secret
　　(—*God's*—) intention
　　rides with the fire, and the clouds, and the ghost
seated in time before eternity is a thing of . . . expulsion, is it?
　　. . . constellation? Thrown
　　　　　　　　out so to be
pieced back together again? So to be
　　worthless and waiting for the fullness of meaning
to arrive. Isn't that a sign? The moon

is a corpse. As is
a house, as is
    a temple. Is a raised

                            (—empty?/empty.—)
glass done
    up to be a grail. Is a grail. The horses drink in
the moon
    -light and the moon
-light shivers and breaks and re-
                            collects in
    the flashing troughs (light from light from light
from light), a memory. What is done. And a symbol.
    Symbol,
meaning "with" and "throw." The horses departed
    into the dark back pastures, leaving me (their hoof
-prints) in the path. I followed. We have been thrown
    together

KATIE FORD

Iridescent Lake

for S & E

After many years, it occurred to me to write of my friends,
of their long marriage,

of the woman who woke one morning
to find an elk had laid down on their porch for the night
to sleep like some heft of creation
ambled out from prehistoric woods,

of how no man or woman had the language evolved enough
to articulate the elk's calligraphic intricacy of heart, nor
what wish might arrive for them, late in age, marriage-old
under blankets worn by the dawn lighting
her blond-grey hair into an almost-likeness of sunrise
on Iridescent Lake,

of some form of yourself you love best because it survived pain that came
like a cornered dog baring its teeth under the same porch
of our elk in this story, the same porch
of the created world resting awhile
on the stoop of this marriage.

Inside, it is Sun Valley.
Her husband spoons sticky rice
into the middle of the bowl,

displacing soup up the sides
with the equivalency pleasure teaches us is pleasure,

just as their bodies pressed the lake
edged in thimbleberry up and up
until it was thinly watered
by his body and hers, the body she kissed
and now kisses, the body she fucked and now fucks,
the body she swims to here in the marriage
of a hundred lakes—Tahoe, Rainier, Iridescent—
and on the Colorado Plateau rivered
as if only for them,

he who labored
to reconvene some semblance of justice for schoolchildren
so shat upon by this country of fat wolves,
she who stripped back violent thought
written by the white minds of men
for a decade, alone at the library carrel
where her heart scholared, too—.

So now we understand the tenderness
with which he spoons rice into the center of her bowl,
why she would say to anything that pains him,
you are thin, you are dirty, then tend it until it is removed
by its own thickened, cleaner ability to live well
and leave her husband alone,

though it's true they've hurt each other and November hurt them both,
they said so, separately, to me: *November.*

But the elk, who had every choice in the forest,
walked out of thin Klimt birch and wild scotchbroom
to sleep at the door
where these two slept.

Opening the door to feel for the weather but to find this elk,
who wouldn't open
all of the way
to that which halts us
to begin, once again, again.

If this were a symbol, I wouldn't brave it as an elk.
It was exactly, and only, an elk.

ALLISON BENIS WHITE
The Track

Of course it is the absence
that is so beautiful.

Human or animal, the snow
will fall and cover her
tracks.

Maybe each word
is a footprint filling up
with snow.

I was here, meaning
I am disappearing.

ALLISON BENIS WHITE

The Shades

At first glance, the trunk
in the river looks like a body
floating face down, naked.

After you died, I saw
you everywhere, which is not
uncommon. Several times a day,
I'd say to myself, Her eyes
(skin, hands) like yours.

I'd say to myself, But not you,
until everyone became more
and more not you, until you were
no one, nowhere—meaning
everyone, everywhere.

SUSANNAH NEVISON

Prisoner's Tubal Ligation with the Archangel Gabriel

The warden comes down
like Gabriel with news
of the Lord that you are
blessed among women
and opens the door to the cell
you keep, the blessed door
of the tomb you keep, unearths
you with news and leads you,
among women, to a room
where God waits in blue
gloves with men who
lower their instruments
in the light of the Lord,
the city of the Lord within
you, blessed among cities,
an instrument of God.
And God's men have come
to fell the soft scaffolding,
so that you, who *know not*
a man, may know only
your body as God's
empty room, an empty
tomb you keep, so that

the warden should come
to your door like Gabriel
with news of the world, the war,
with the blinding light
of the Lord just out of reach.

STEVEN CORDOVA

Kissing Mary M.

I kissed him to move the narrative along
to a climax as messy as any story ending
in human sacrifice.

I kissed him for thirty silver coins. I was poor
& I had walked beside him a long way
from my home.

I kissed him because the devil entered me
& he wanted him, too. The devil wanted him
most of all.

I kissed him, betrayed him as he betrayed me:
He thought I hadn't seen him, but I had:
He was kissing Mary M.

WESLEY ROTHMAN

Transubstantiation

Where light bruises the air
Discreetly, time turns to smoke. Walk
Through & it dominates.
                  Passing a mirror
I catch the curve of an ear, a foreign
Gait, how the right shoulder dips more deeply
Than the left. I turn my hand in the air
& the vein that writhes is not mine. I know,
Somehow, it is that of a man I've seen
Only in photos.
                In one he stands nearby
My mother. I lean against his left leg
Just grown enough to wobble. Wherever
We stand, the light is remnant—low glow
Of a hushed wick.
                & there, his face is not his,
Nor his gut. He has become his great-
Grandfather, whose hand commands the over-
Seer. Smoke trails litter the valley there,
Fields purple with ground fog, ripen with blood.
& here my blood loops, smoke in that light.

CAROL POTTER

Stealth, or A Sweet Bit of Stealing

She said she loved me. She was a mink stole.
A girl stole. The stole between her legs. Her breasts
stole me, her mouth had me. She and I stole from each
other. We drove to another state and the state
stole from us. Jesus stole something. There were signs
along the roadway: *Jesus Saves*. We were stealing
ourselves quietly by ourselves so no one could see.
There were cicadas stealing the silence from the air.
Stealing our words. Cracking them together between
their legs. We were stealing the state. We got stolen
from. There were bees in the apples stealing
sweet meat from the trees. There were apples on
the ground stealing dirt from the earth. There
were stealers stealing around us singing their bird
songs. There was a flood and a stealing stinging
bee sting. She stung me. I loved her. She stole and I stole
from her. She loved me. It was a sweet bit of stealing.
A nickel. A dime. A few years. Some bird song.

KAI CARLSON-WEE

Party Barn

In the middle of the empty field the barn stands abandoned.
I duck through the broken door, letting my vision adjust
to the inner dark. Bottles of Grain Belt litter
the floorboards. Corn-pipes. Condoms. Marlboro Reds.
Straw from the gone swallows' nests.
Fourteen years since I last came
back here. Same bad graffiti. Same crooked staircase
leading me up to the loft. Rafter-beams over me,
scoring the night sky, eaten away
by wind. I don't know what becomes of love.
What purple scroll of rolling smoke
still hungers for a kiss. A thousand dead stars
leaking their false light. Freight trains riding the miles
of soybeans here to the fracking lands west.
Your breasts in the summer air. Dull light of satellites
stitching the uncut corn. I don't know why the distance
makes it more. Why time allows this
ruined barn to bloom. Why all those nights are clearer now.
The smell of sweat and gathered dust. Mud tracks
of the river's touch. Skin we knew entirely by moon.

ANDERS CARLSON-WEE

Old Church

Haunted so we didn't follow him
inside. Posing at a broken window
he thumbed the dusty pages, preaching
like our dad. Between passages
he puffed his cheeks and wormed
his fat tongue between forked fingers.
This is what your mom worships,
he said. We never told him to stop,
just started chucking rocks from the fence.
First at the shards of stained glass
gummed in the frame like shark teeth.
Then at him. Then at him harder,
his face popping up between our fire
like a self-winding jack-in-the-box.
The bad throw that connected
ricocheted so we didn't see, just heard
our cousin scream. We froze, bracing
for darkness to burst out the door
and roar toward us. But it didn't.
The heavy hinges creaked and Scott
stumbled out holding his lowered head,
pleading for help. At ten years old
I was ready for rage, even death,
even ghosts. But not this: his blond hair
bright with blood, his real moan.

Nonfiction

CAROL D. MARSH

How to Build a Bonfire

*P*ICK A SAFE SPOT.

    The slight depression with its darkened earth, bits of blackened twigs and surrounding stones lies near but not too close to the maple tree, halfway between house and cow barn. He passes that bit of ground every day. Not as often as he used to, when milking cows morning and night for sixty-plus years, yet regularly, on his way to the barn out of habit or to check in with his son before he takes the tractor to tend something in one of the fields. His wife comes with him as she's been doing for about a year, ever since she became frightened when she can't see him. As they walk across the yard together on this late summer day, he thinks about a bonfire and begins to plan. The stump of that dead tree he had cut down this summer would do nicely. And there's always brush to clear, as well as accumulated stuff in the barn and woodshed. He slows his pace a bit, realizing she's behind him, anxious, unsure of her footing on the uneven ground and afraid she'll look up and he'll be gone.

Find tinder (small twigs, bark), kindling (larger sticks and branches), and fuel (logs and large wood objects no longer needed).

He uses the tractor to yank the old stump out of the ground and drag it over to where bonfires have burned for decades. It anchors the growing pile of tangled brush cleared from the hedgerow on the road by the pasture where cows used to graze. He likes to start gathering brush long before bonfire day so the branches, sere and brown, will pop and crackle, embers erupting. Newspapers are ready by the woodshed door. No sense putting them out early, if it rains the resulting sodden mess would never dry in time. With them are milk cartons, paper bags, accumulated junk from the garage, and even two of those wide strips of rubber mat on which the cows slept in their stalls. That big bag of old twine gets placed near the barn door.

Stepping just inside the garage, he hesitates before the wooden crib in which all five of his children slept until the youngest graduated to a bed in 1966. His daughters had hauled it to the garage when clearing out the first floor bedroom a month ago. That room became the master bedroom because neither he nor his wife does stairs well any more. His knee is bad and requires surgery that will mean weeks of rehab and impaired mobility. And he's fearful of her increasing disorientation. What if she falls down the stairs in nighttime wanderings? The crib has been replaced by a dresser. But neither he nor his daughters have had the heart to haul it to the dump.

Though he's not known for outward sentimentality, he hesitates. He's alone right now in ability to imagine a future and understand the import of the past, yet all his life he's made such decisions as a farmer does: everything that can be re-used or re-engineered for new service in house or barn is valuable and needed. The rest is disposed of.

He hauls the crib out to the growing pile.

Continuing to gather and place combustibles.

The stump is now invisible under a confusion of branches, brown leaves and old wood. She loves helping when he scouts the yard and its edges for farm detritus—clumps of dead weeds, old corn cobs, nuts fallen from the black walnut tree. The effort calms her with its companionship and back-and-forth of pulling dead stuff from the yard's rough border, carrying it to the pile, tossing it on then turning to look for more. It had been the same when the old tree was cut down and chopped. In a rare attitude of peace, she'd fallen into the rhythm of his steady purpose, understanding the idea of making an orderly pile from the tumble of freshly cut logs, and pleased with that understanding. The two of them, not needing to speak, moved to and fro between diminishing chaos and growing order, coordination of this sort having become effortless in the sixty years since they were teenagers and just married. He wonders if she knows this chopped-up tree was the one that held the roped tire swing. Five kids played on that swing and ran around the yard under her watchful eye out the kitchen window.

Watch the weather

He hopes the weather will hold, but the forecast is iffy. It might rain, like it did two days ago, making him wonder if his care to collect and dry the fuel early has gone for nothing. He waits it out, hoping for better weather but knowing it's out of his control. She's still asking, every time the two of them go outdoors, what the pile is for. She remembers making the log structure, but the seemingly random litter for the fire makes no sense to her. He usually responds patiently, but patience can come hard to a man accustomed to working independently within a partnership of trust and mutual, unspoken values. She who had shared responsibility is now merely following him, and what used to be the combined if separate efforts of two strong and self-reliant people has morphed into his singleness of responsibility for her. It's better when she has a small job to do, one that's soothing in its repetition, but those tasks are done for now and there's nothing to replace them.

On bonfire day, get an early start shaping the pile so it's high with a broad base; it should be ready to light by mid-morning.

By 8:00 am, he's outdoors with a rake, scraping the edges of the pile upward and inward into the pyramid shape that's optimal for producing hot, long-lasting coals. The fuel is dry, the rain having lasted only half a day. He doesn't stop to check wind direction; he knows it like he knows a coming change in weather, not something he must think about, just an awareness. He grabs the bag of twine and props it against the windward side of the pyramid. Then come the newspapers, dry and dusty, some to be spread on top of the bag, the rest over everything else. The pile sags under their weight.

Light the fire

He crouches next to the bag of twine, holding a long-necked lighter. The breeze is strong enough to threaten the tiny flame, but he touches it to the bag where it's sheltered by his body. Orange tongues curl around and up. He comes out of the crouch stiffly, accommodating knees that have bent and held and straightened at the sides of countless cows, every day twice a day since he was sixteen and legally old enough to leave school. The wind blows over it all. A shower of sparks follows the growing flames with a satisfying crackle and hiss. When he's sure the blaze is strong, one that will last hours, he goes to the log pile ten feet away. Carrying a short, fat log in each hand, he strides over to the fire, pauses a moment, then thrusts them assuredly into the flames. He turns back to the log pile.

She comes out of the house with her daughter-in-law, happy to see him working at the rows of chopped wood the two of them stacked, ten logs high and two logs deep. As before, she falls into the rhythm of the work, imitating his movement and toggling between fire and log pile, chatting aimlessly and smiling.

Tend the fire

The fire must be watched as it goes its fierce, hot way. Left alone, it will burn too fast and die, falling in on itself. Every half-hour or so he walks its perimeter, kicking logs that have rolled away back toward the center. He bends to pick up corncobs scattered under the trees, dropped by squirrels after they have eaten the kernels off. He rakes bark that has peeled off the logs. It's all fuel. When he's in the house getting lunch, he looks out the window above the sink to monitor the height of the flames and the direction of the smoke. Next to him, she puzzles about how to slice tomatoes.

Eleven years before, he spoke into a microphone in the hall rented for their fiftieth anniversary party. They wanted him to make a speech, the people sitting at round tables covered with white cloths and the remnants of buffet dinners, they clapped and laughed. So he went to the mic but didn't start the speech right away. He looked for her. He said she had stood by him for fifty years and he wanted her beside him now. Then he didn't speak for long moments: it may have been the catch in his voice that silenced him, or he may have been watching her come to him. Now she's at his side constantly in a way that's cruel mockery of his meaning that night. It's not what he had hoped for their last years together, not remotely what he imagined sixty-one years ago, in love with her joy and warmth and flaming red hair. But it's what life has given the two of them, in the same way it sometimes gave too much rain and sometimes too little so that, year to year, they learned to accept the uncertainty and manage together as well as they could.

Ensure hot, long-lasting coals

The fire burns. The rake leans against the oak, ready to be grabbed if the pile collapses outside the circle of stones. He's vigilant at the fire's side, knowing the only way to get lasting coals—the kind that cook the meat through, glowing on into the evening well past the marshmallow roast—is to shape it and watch it and shape it again. It's a cloudy day, but not raining.

Two hours before supper, he finally allows the cone to settle into its middle, insulating and protecting the glowing coals beneath.

Welcome the guests

He hasn't even told her there's to be a party, keeping preparations out of her sight. But she has begun to suspect something's up. He tries to reassure her but she becomes restless, worried there is something she's supposed to do but unsure what it is or how to do it. When people arrive they don't bring presents, just cards, which they put discreetly on the dining room table. No one knows how she might react to finding out it's his birthday, but, given the panic attack before the previous family party, no one wants to find out. She wanders in and out of the rooms, a bit calmer now that guests distract her from pressing yet unknown responsibilities, smiling and talking to people she cannot name, some of whom she's known all her life and three of whom she bore.

Three months later

He stands at the kitchen window, staring out over the yard and thinking about her. She lives a few miles away in the home that, unbelievably, she now needs more than she needs him. He has survived failed crops and a near-deadly tractor accident, family illnesses and deaths, blizzards, bad knees and sick cows. He has watched the sky and walked the fields and known it's not he who makes it work but the two of them together and the light of their faith in all that is good and sacred. The house feels so very empty. Outside in the yard, halfway to the cow barn and near but not too close to the maple, where bits of blackened twigs lie amidst fallen leaves, a wisp of smoke seems to rise to the sky.

Admission

"I HATE THIS SONG. IT DOESN'T MAKE any sense."

A friend of mine and I have just had dinner, having gotten together for the first time since she's moved here to Missouri. We're sitting in my parked car talking when I notice the song playing. "I paid for Sirius once I realized there weren't any black stations. I got tired of listening to Taylor Swift all the time, but this isn't much better. It's not even a good rap song."

"Kevin Gates," she says, laughing. "His rap name even sucks! Santana is a better rap name and he isn't even a rapper." She pulls out her phone, searches for the lyrics. She recites them, jokingly imitating a poet persona for fun. After she finishes and both of us have quieted down from laughing, I change the subject.

"I'm sorry I haven't been around," I say, wondering if she can hear my guilt. "After the protests on campus—I just decided I couldn't be around anymore."

"At least everything seems to be settling down for now," she says.

"Have you seen—" I begin before stopping myself, unsure if I should ask.

"He asked about you," she says, answering my question. It was not hard for her to guess who I was referring to since there are only a few of us here in this program.

"What did he say? I haven't talked to him since the start of the semester, since before everything happened. I guess we got into it."

"He just seemed concerned as all. I think he thought you were upset with him."

"Yeah, well," I say, then shrug.

I pause, thinking back to what happened. He was angry at the department's lack of response. It doesn't affect most of them so they don't care, he'd told me. He was frustrated at my cohort, at their apathy. I'm the only one who has to worry about being shot as a black man, he'd said.

For a while he sent out emails forwarded to the entire department, calling on them to put action to their words. Email after email was blasted off, the effect of which causing increasing hostility in response. He eventually decided he wanted to do a boycott, sending out an email to the handful of us in the program.

You've got to stop this. I'd finally messaged. *You're just making everyone angry.*

That's a good thing, he'd quickly written back.

Why are you doing this? What about school?

This is important, he answered, then stopped responding to my messages.

His proposed boycott dissipated before it could start, most of us were too occupied with just making it through school to deal with anything else.

I'd thought a lot about his response since. He was so sure, so forceful in what he felt was the right thing to do, even at the risk of potential backlash. In contrast, I remembered my father's response on the night I told him about the protests—you are there to work, remember? You are there to get your degree and get out, don't lose sight of that goal. I thought of the ways I had spent my life attempting to erase markers of my blackness until I did not know who I was anymore. I thought of how, even still, the night of the threats I'd sat in my car afraid to start the engine, and I thought of how after, when for a moment the world had seemed to settle down, while walking down the street I was yelled a slur and even then my first instinct was to let it go, to bury it, to ignore the fact that it happened.

You can be good. You can be accommodating. You can make the world comfortable with your blackness as so many of us try to in our daily lives. You can straighten your hair, code-switch, be quiet instead of speaking out, and yet one day you may still find yourself confronted with a group of men, wild-eyed and in a frenzy, who will shout slurs at you, and you will be reminded in the end that in this world it doesn't matter how good you are.

"I should probably get in touch with him," I finally say. In the quiet I reach over and shift to a new station, this one plays D'Angelo. My friend laughs.

"Come on D'Angelo," she says upon hearing the first few verses. "Calling yourself the Black Messiah, as if all of us have forgotten about the time when all anyone cared about was seeing your dick. No one forgot. I still remember."

We both laugh. It's nice sitting in the car with her, the two of us having this moment.

"You know, I feel responsible for encouraging you to come here," I finally admit. "I'm sorry if you've had a hard time."

"It's okay. It hasn't been that bad. I mean, up until now."

"Have you been doing okay?"

She pauses, thinks about my question. "Yeah, someone called me a slur at the beginning of the semester but since things have been fine."

"It happens," I say, and because I am nearing the end of my time here and she's at the beginning, I don't tell her I've been called slurs too, multiple times, and between the both of us it will most likely happen again.

"I'm used to it. Once in school the teacher read out loud *Huck Finn* and kept emphasizing all the slurs. He read them over and over while the rest of class just stared at me. Later, the teacher came up and was like, 'oh, I didn't realize, this didn't bother you, did it?'"

"Seriously?"

"Must be nice to go through your life like that—offending people and not worrying about it until afterward." She pauses. "It doesn't matter, they're just words. I tried telling my parents about it, what with it and then with the protests, and they didn't understand."

"I know what you mean. My father went to school the year after Wilmington Ten," I say, remembering the story of what happened. In February of 1971 in Wilmington, North Carolina, tensions over school desegregation had reached a breaking point. Four days of violence rocked the town, resulting in two deaths and the firebombing of a white-owned store. The National Guard had to come in to restore the peace. The Wilmington Ten were a group of students convicted of arson and conspiracy to fire upon firemen and police officers. They were sentenced to 282 years in prison. After their sentence, a movement formed in the state demanding their freedom.

"So it's like," I say, continuing. "I call my father up sometimes and I'll say—well, so and so said this, or this happened, and he'll be like, 'so what's the problem? Your *feelings* were hurt? Is that why you're calling?'"

"It's the price of admission for being here," she says, and I nod.

"You know, I'm thinking about writing about all this—a bunch of essays about race." I then explain about my family, about their history. I tell her I'm thinking of going to Louisiana, of visiting the Whitney Museum, the first plantation dedicated to the memory of slavery. "My ancestors were all on tobacco plantations, not so much cotton or sugar like in the Deep South, but I still feel as if I have to go and see the ones there, especially the Whitney. Who knows if anything will come from it but I'm gonna go. The time's there, better make use before it's gone."

"I went to a lot of them for my novel," she tells me. "We went to one that had an intact slave cabin and it was so hot I almost passed out, but I thought—this was how it was, they were working in this heat, and so I pulled myself together."

"Those plantations are something else."

"I know, so many columns."

"That Greek Revival architecture."

"All built on the backs of slaves."

"I've never talked about race before," I suddenly say, thinking about this book and my hesitancy to write it. "I always thought if I avoided it maybe others wouldn't see me as different."

It has taken me years to get to this confession, it has taken me most of my life. Saying it out loud feels as if I am reaching closer, that I am slowly reclaiming back my sense of self.

"People are going to see you that way though. No matter what they want to pretend."

She has already gotten to a place I am still struggling to reach. I don't respond, don't know how to, and for the first time during our evening we both have settled into silence.

"Oh, here we go." I motion to the new song on the radio. Beyonce's *Formation* has just started playing. "I used to be so critical of her, but now I don't know what to think. What about you? Do you think she's being authentic with this album? That her video is pandering?"

"I don't know. Maybe. I'm not sure how much it matters though."

I don't know this answer either, but what I wonder is how I would have felt had I heard this when I was younger—to witness such an affirmation of blackness, and even though my heart skips a moment, a tinge of nervousness, of insecurity from others around us passing by, I roll the windows down anyway, and let the music fill the air.

Chasing the Cantaloupe Man

I PAID TOO MUCH TO STAY THE night in a bad motel in Nuevo Casas Grandes and woke grateful for morning, for I knew the cure for a bad Mexican night is a good Mexican breakfast. And the night had been bad, crossing the border at Agua Prieta late afternoon, dodging the potholes across the Sonoran and then the Chihuahuan deserts to Janos, pulling into Nuevo Casas Grandes after the last restaurant on the highway had closed.

The room at Las Fuentes reeked of disinfectant, and the pillow, a plastic bag filled with stale cubes of foam, crunched with my every move. The air conditioner, stuck loosely in the wall, worked only on "fan," a small square of dirty duct tape stuck across the low and hi cool buttons. The fan rattled and mightily roared. Something, a leaf, or perhaps a desiccated rat's tail, had caught in the blower and flapped and fluttered all night. In my half-sleep I was a young boy furiously pedaling my bike while the spokes of the rear wheel fought against the square of cardboard I had clothes-pinned to a fender brace. But the fan did pull the dry Chihuahuan desert night air through the room and by the cool hours of early morning brought some relief.

At first light I found the motel office empty, and the television on. I glanced up to find Daffy Duck in black and white speaking Spanish. To my surprise—and regret—I understood most of it. The coffee pot sat dry and cold, so I cruised the little town with my pickup windows rolled down.

I had been through Nuevo Casas Grandes more than once before and remembered a small cafe on a side street, a place where on another trip into Mexico a few years back I had found coffee and breakfast. A woman worked the kitchen, and a man I took to be her husband smoked and read a day-old *periodico*. They acted as if a gringo customer was not out of the ordinary and welcome, and that pleased me. I recalled the cafe first of all as clean and bright, and second for its breakfast, two golden high-yolked eggs smothered with *pico de gallo*, the onions and tomatoes roughly chopped and tossed with a sprinkling of cilantro, and thin rounds of fresh serrano peppers. I sat at the counter and watched the woman hand-pat corn tortillas, thick and moist, and grill them on a blackened *comal*. They held the flavor of corn, fresh off the cob. Tortillas you could taste, would remember.

This morning it took only a few minutes to zigzag the downtown streets, but the cafe had disappeared. Or I had become completely disoriented. Disappointed, I picked up the highway south, hungry, but mostly regretting that I had no coffee, and headed for Buenaventura, an hour or so away.

A sack beside me held emergency rations and I stuck one hand in deep and felt around: a jar of dry roasted peanuts, a package of honey-something granola bars, a bag of lemon drops. I would wait. I knew that an early lunch could be had in three or so hours, before I reached Cuauhtémoc, the next sizeable city. There, along a straight stretch of road with modern farms and houses and enormous barns on either side, I would pass through miles of *rubios* country, Mennonite communities that had coexisted prosperously in that part of Mexico for decades. There, in every store and market, I would find cheese, a half-dozen varieties both fresh and aged, sold by blond women and their daughters who spoke Spanish to me, but whispered in an undecipherable foreign old-country tongue when I wandered away.

Each dairy along the highway made its own cheeses. Some, similar to queso fresco and traditional farmers' cheeses, crumbled when sliced, while others had the smooth consistency of Gouda. The Mennonites do not dye their cheeses, and use unpasteurized raw milk straight from their Guernsey or Holstein herds, but I had faith in the cleanliness of the cheese makers, and many times had sampled my way through that soft, very un-Mexican country. If I could keep myself from the granola bars until I got there I would pick up a box of saltines and an apple, and with a couple of kinds of cheese make a tasty lunch.

At Buenaventura I turned back to the west, away from the direction that led eventually to the city of Chihuahua. A small *zocalo* marks the spot where the road splits east and west, the *zocalo* laid out as a small rectangular plaza with the main road running along one side and a few unremarkable office buildings and stores enclosing the others. Unremarkable for the most part, but on one corner I spotted a bakery, "Lulu's" written in lavish blue script across the display window. I stopped.

The bakery was small, but crammed with pastries of all kinds. On this day a special cake held center stage, a dozen or more of them on a table in the center of the room. The cakes swirled with patterns and flowers, topped with small childlike, thumb-sized dolls, in anticipation of the Day of the Children, which was upcoming later in the week.

In Mexico nothing outside the cities and large towns' "super mercados" is packaged or kept behind the counter. Lulu's was no exception. I took a round metal tray from a stack—it was very much like an extra-large pizza pan—and grabbed a pair of tongs. I moved from biscuits to cookies to empanadas to cupcakes, and used the tongs to load my tray, operating on the pure impulse of hunger. The woman behind the counter, Lulu, I suppose, watched with a friendly, but bemused expression.

In a few minutes I slid the heaping tray across to her and she filled a white paper sack, handling the tongs as if she were a time and motion expert. She tallied the prices out loud as she went. All too quick for me to follow, But the total was ridiculously low. "*Café*?" I asked, without much hope. She shrugged with a smile and shook her head.

Back in the truck I continued east, crossing the Santa Maria River. The mountains rose ahead so I decided to try the pastries while still on a stretch of straight road. Disappointing. The cupcakes crumbled dryly into my lap, and needed more sugar for my taste. Ditto for the cookies. Flour must be inexpensive, I figured, and butter and eggs and sugar more pricey. I know my pastries, know my butter and sugar and eggs, know too well what they can do. But Buenaventura is a tiny agricultural town and Lulu's customers will buy what they can afford and no more. Lulu did quite well, I conceded, given her resources and the resources of her daily clientele. And maybe less rich, less moist in pastries was an acquired taste. Dipped in coffee they might not be bad at all. Certainly superior to the Bimbo brand, Twinkie-imitation products that are trucked from huge plants in the cities to small *tiendas* all over Mexico.

A few miles east of Buenaventura the road narrowed and began to climb sharply and I found myself navigating a series of switchbacks that would lead up and over the Sierra la Catarina and then on down to the town of Zaragosa in the next valley. It was still early and I expected little traffic, had, in fact, chosen this route to avoid the trucks that move so aggressively from El Paso to and from points south. I had taken this route a couple of years before, knew it to be narrow and winding, with many *CURVA PELIGROSA* signs, but with a little luck I could be back down to a straight and slightly wider road in an hour or so.

Around the next corner, almost before I realized it, I came upon a pick-up truck, a mid-sixties vintage Chevrolet, its bed loaded with cantaloupes. A band of red and blue fringe dangled across the interior length of the truck's windshield, whipping in the wind from the open windows. The name, MIGUEL, took up the width of the tailgate, boldly written in fancy script.

Miguel spotted me early on; I could see his eyes move from the road ahead then back to the rearview mirror, but there were no pull-offs, and I stayed back a decent distance, so not to crowd him on the mountainous road. He appeared to be young, drove with one hand on the wheel while propping his other arm out the open window, and gave no inclination to ease to the right or slow and let me pass. And once, when I had a short window of opportunity before me on a rare level stretch of road, he gave the old truck all it had and with a plume of black smoke and a roar from a holey muffler he left me in his dust. My Ford Ranger is fairly new, but with four cylinders underpowered for this terrain, and even if he had slowed, I hardly had the guts to pass him on one of the short straightaways that ended so abruptly in blind curves. So we struggled on for a few miles.

By the way Miguel drove, the way he kept his eye on me in his outside mirror, I could guess his intentions, almost hear him say, "No way a rich gringo will pass me." Despite my best attempt to maintain a gentle and kind attitude, I could feel my deep-seated, almost tribal response, "We'll see, we'll see."

So the chase was on. He left me on downhill stretches, taking curves without touching his brakes, it seemed, although soon, as his heavy load pushed him down that mountain, I could smell the truck's brakes hot and smoking, and I concluded that he did have brakes, but no brake lights.

On long climbs, by aggressively gearing down, I could catch him once more and sense his frustration as I crept closer to his bumper than I would have normally dared. To the left a drop-off with no guardrails and a *descanso,* three grey wooden crosses with faded plastic flowers, wedged into a pile of rocks. Then at the crest of the hill once more he took control and sped down, dodging potholes and on around a bend where he disappeared. Somewhere ahead of me the blat-blat-blat of the Chevy echoed off the rocky slopes, until the road turned up and I could slowly pull in behind him again.

Through it all the melons pyramided in the back of his truck miraculously held in place. The cantaloupes for the most part were small, splotchy with sunburned spots and misshapen. But I could smell them, their unmistakable freshness, their ripeness, in the same way that last fall I had driven through apple country on another trip into Mexico and been almost overcome by the sweetness of the harvest.

Back home in Tucson during the past month I had tried to find a flavorful cantaloupe. Safeway had some beauties, extra-large with uniform coloration and nicely patterned webs all around. They embodied perfection, as if they had never touched a sandy field nor seen the sun.

Perfection, except for their flavor. When cut, the cantaloupe color was right, a uniform golden, but the flesh was hard and I could hardly scoop it out with a spoon. The flavor wasn't bad, it just wasn't. Bred for a world market, they were thick-skinned, picked green and shipped—the mantra of American agri-business.

I remembered a time as a boy, back in east Texas where I grew up. It was summertime, like now, and I had gone with my dad out to a farmer's house. I must have been about twelve, for I remember being embarrassed when my dad didn't step up onto the front porch and knock, but stood out front in the swept yard "helloing" the house until the farmer finally heard him and joined us in the bright sun.

While the men talked the three of us and a couple of hounds wandered slowly into the field that had been planted almost up to the yard. Watermelons lay everywhere, nestled heavy in the blow-sand. Glistening, solid green ones and long zigzagged striped ones and pale green round ones that hid their yellow hearts. The farmer hitched the knees of his overalls and knelt beside a melon, thumped it a couple of times and moved on. When he found one he liked he simply lifted the melon waist high and dropped it, cracking it open. Then with his pocketknife he carved out only the heart of the melon and offered a dripping piece to me and another to my dad. We moved on, working our way around bull nettles and patches of grass burrs to two or three more melons, different varieties, each one hot and sweet and bursting with flavor. We ate only the heart of each and left the broken halves in the field to the bees and yellow jackets, the squirrels and raccoons. The best melons I have ever tasted, and that pretty well ruined me for the supermarket variety of today.

Still I tailed Miguel's pickup of melons as we crept over the mountain pass and entered a sweeping straightaway that led into the valley. There, Miguel caught my eye in his rearview mirror. He gave me a little wave and he and his load of cantaloupes left me behind. I didn't even try to keep up.

When the road finally leveled off and Zaragosa came in sight, I spotted the Chevy truck ahead, parked off the road on an open patch of gravel. I slowed and pulled in behind the sagging truck, not too close. Miguel had propped the truck's hood open with a stick. He sloshed a milk bottle of water towards the radiator, then jumped back from a surge of steam and smoke. He saw me and grinned, as if to ask, "What took you so long?"

I eased out of the truck, and hobbled around to loosen up. I wandered over to check his load of cantaloupes. Some were a little overripe, a few had been bruised in handling. But they all passed my sniff test. This would be breakfast. "How much?" I asked in my best Spanish.

"For all?" he responded, his eyes lighting up.

"For one. Or maybe two."

Miguel laughed and moved his hands across in front of his body as if I had slid safely into home plate just ahead of the ball. "For nothing," he said. "I have many. You can see."

I offered him five pesos, at that time about sixty cents, but he wouldn't take my money. Miguel picked out two nice melons and handed them to me. "These are good," he said. "From my father's own land."

I lowered the tailgate of my pickup and pulled out my pocket knife. The cantaloupe cut smooth and quiet. I raked the seeds out of one half, scattering them across the gravel, and dug in.

The meat was firm without being hard, infused with an indescribable sweetness. I felt as if I could stay there for the morning and put away half of his truckload. What a Californian would pay for one of these, I thought.

I cut the other half in wedges and offered one to Miguel. He put his hand to his stomach. "*Muchos melones*," he said. He motioned west, toward Zaragosa. "If I sell them all for a good price in Zaragosa, maybe I will find a *hamburguesa* there." He shrugged and slid into his truck. "But if not, I always have my mama's beans and tortillas." In a moment he fired up the truck and with a roar he was gone.

I sat there on the tailgate of my truck and finished both melons. I remembered a time near Uruapan, way south in Michoacán, the heart of avocado country, peeling an avocado picked fresh from a tree with this same knife, with this same pleasure. And I remembered another time sampling six varieties of bananas at a roadside stand as I neared Puerto Ángel on a drive from Oaxaca City to the coast. Six kinds. I couldn't get over it. Just picked that morning, not green, but ripe from the trees.

Then I thought of the markets scattered all over Mexico, where each stall holds colorful, carefully stacked pyramids and baskets of fresh produce of all kinds. But where now, more and more, each of these stalls also holds a tiny television set, where the women (mostly) who run the stalls watch whatever beams their way from Mexico City or Monterrey or Guadalajara, bringing something into the air of the markets that contaminates the atmosphere, makes me uneasy. Something foreign, alien to the places, television with pitches for dried milk and canned fruit-like juices and boxes of sugared, colorful cereals, for processed meats and sliced Bimbo bread.

I remembered those apples I had eaten last fall south of Saltillo, and being concerned about another sort of contamination. The apples weren't red delicious, but smaller, rounder, picked ripe that morning from a roadside orchard, bursting with all that unforgettable flavor. But I carefully peeled those apples, worrying about pesticides and the lax Mexican laws, about the way chemical companies all over the globe see Mexico as just another unprotected market for sprays that our own country has banned,

How many truckloads of cantaloupes did Miguel haul from his father's field each year? Three or maybe four? And when his father no longer works his field, when farming has "progressed" into agri-business, what then? Will Miguel be content to work the small field each year? Probably not, and perhaps he shouldn't. But where will vine-ripened cantaloupes, those varieties unsuitable for long distant shipping be found? And selfishly I wondered, where will I find them?

I slammed the tailgate of my truck, wiped the knife on my jeans and in a panic pulled back on the empty highway and raced towards Zaragosa. There, I turned off the main road and eased up and down each dusty street, searching for Miguel and his pickup, hoping to find it still heavy with melons. I glanced back at the bed of my own truck. Empty. If I could find Miguel and his cantaloupes, I would buy them all.

JOSEPH LAPIN

When Dogs Run Away

HEN A DOG SLIPS OUT OF a collar and runs toward a busy street, the instinct is to chase after it like a madman, screaming at the dog to stop. At this point, it's impossible to reason with the dog, but in the moment, it seems plausible that a command can convince the dog to halt. Take for instance the other day when I arrived at my office in Ocean Beach, San Diego: With an acai bowl toppling over with strawberries, frozen bananas, and honey in one hand and a latte in the other, I opened the door and saw our office dog Layla, a fifty-pound Australian shepherd, and a new dog Penelope, a skittish Maltese that weighed close to five pounds. As soon as I opened the door, Layla bit poor Penelope in the ass. Seeing an opportunity, Penelope booked it and ran straight toward the street at a pace comparable to an Impala trying to run away from a hungry cheetah. So, instinctively, I started running, too.

"Penelope," I yelled. "Please, stop."

Just recently a group of researchers published a study in the American Association for the Advancement of Science to understand how dogs process meaning in speech. According to *PBS NewsHour*, "It took [the] team months to train six border collies, five golden retrievers, a German shepherd and a Chinese crested to remain still as their brains were scanned." What they learned is that dogs process language similar to human beings, and through a combination of intonation and language, dogs can comprehend their owners.

But in my experience, when dogs run away, language ceases to have any power. The intonation of a scared owner sounds panicked, and a dog can't process the words accurately. They can't decipher that "Stop" means "If you run into the street, then you're going to die." Clearly, Penelope was confused somewhere between my intonation and word choice, and she ran down the

NONFICTION

stairs of our office and straight into the intersection on Cable and Bacon, where cars often come dangerously close to killing people walking toward the Ocean Beach pier.

"Penelope, stop," I yelled, imagining her flattened like a penny left on a train track. How was I going to explain to the owner, a friend who loved Penelope like it was her child, that her dog had been run over by a jeep with two surfboards strapped on the top rack driven by a guy who hopped out and said: "Sorry about your dog, bro"?

I ran faster, spilling the coffee and the fruit, knowing that my entire office was watching from the windows above the OB Noodle House. To my luck, a family on bicycles approached the intersection instead of a cadre of cars and trucks revving their engines, and they tried to corner the dog, but Penelope was evasive, scooting away from their outstretched hands, and I tried to grab her, feeling like Rocky Balboa chasing after a chicken to build up footspeed as he prepared to fight Apollo Creed. Finally, I put the acai bowl and the latte on the ground and had Penelope stopped in her tracks, but she fled to the undercarriage of a Jeep Cherokee. So I moved behind the Jeep, hoping that I could grab her by the collar, dragging her back to the place she tried so desperately to run from.

But as soon as I moved behind her, she ran back the other way, weaving in and out of the grasping hands of the family on their bicycles. "Penelope. Stop." I could see the shadow of a car moving in the background the way someone might be startled by the sudden presence of a shark appearing while scuba diving. When she moved into the intersection, I saw the boyfriend of Penelope's owner standing in the middle of the road, and as soon as Penelope saw him, she rolled over and submitted, exhausted and tired.

■ ■ ■

What is the proper way to act when a dog runs? Not just any run: That panic run that seems pushed forward by a ghost in their mind, a vision that exists just outside of the human eye. They run like a character in a Tennessee Williams play sprinting toward the road to commit suicide. I want to believe in a precise combination of intonation and language that will force a dog to listen to reason. But I know that doesn't exist, and somehow, against all logic, it's become my duty to try and save the dogs when I see them running.

It's happened countless times. I've seen more dogs lost in the street than I can count, and no matter what I'm doing, whether I'm heading to a job interview or an important meeting, if I see a lost dog, then I must stop. I have a feeling it comes down to my own dog. I have a mutt named Hendrix, and every time I see a dog running down the street I see him heading to some unknowable disaster, too, knowing that I was responsible for his protection.

But sometimes, I've realized, it might be best to let the poor pooch go. For instance, I was leaving a Denis Johnson reading at the University of Southern California, and I was walking alone toward my car that was parked somewhere off campus. I was, in fact, having trouble remembering where I parked. At least it was a warm, summer night, and I couldn't believe how empty the roads were, which made me a bit nervous. The area around USC wasn't known for its safety to say the least.

I pushed the button to cross the street, and the campus glowed behind me like a power plant. I thought about the drive home to Long Beach, where I lived with my wife and dog, knowing that I would have to jump on the 710, eventually, and drive past the cloud factories and the Lego-building block machinery that festered off the 405 like a tick that was gradually sucking the blood out of a city. Even though it defied logic to have bumper-to-bumper on Tuesday at 10 pm, there would be some unexplainable happening like an oil tanker catching fire underneath a bridge, causing congestion. But for the moment, the street was entirely empty.

"Wait, wait, wait," the robotic voice said at the crosswalk.

As the electronic sign changed from a flat, orange hand to a stick figure walking, that's when I saw the brown pit bull running down the middle of the street. For a moment, I wondered if I should seek cover. Perhaps the dog was rabid, and it was just searching for its first victim, but I couldn't turn away; I was transfixed by this dog that was galloping down the middle of the empty L.A. street like a vision I needed to capture some meaning from.

"Dog!" I yelled. "Dog. Dog."

The dog didn't look at me, and I watched the muscular legs and the eyes that looked as wide and bright as it had seen the world after years of living in a cage in a basement. There was no reasoning, I could tell, with this dog. It had already left this world, and if I tried to bring it back, then it might take me with it. The green light turned to red again, and I had to wait at the crosswalk as the mutt ran down the street, further and further into the quiet city.

"Dog!" I yelled. "Dog. Dog."

■ ■ ■

I wonder if I felt bad about judging that dog. But the most important lesson in learning how to run after dogs is comprehending when you can help them—and when help it's impossible. I was trying to atone for that one incident at USC a few years later when I was walking down Barrington Avenue in Brentwood, and it was one of those spectacular days in LA that caused me to wonder if the sky was actually created by CGI. I was headed to grab a coffee on the corner of Barrington and San Vincente, where pretty people stood in line for a $4 beverage, when I heard a car behind me beeping. Not just once. Incessantly. I turned around and saw a Great Dane, his giant paws beating down the crowded Barrington Avenue with the Sunday afternoon traffic, and its leash was dragging behind him.

"Stop," I yelled.

Instinctively, I started running after the dog who was causing the lines of traffic to divert like Jim Carey in *Bruce Almighty*. I bolted down the sidewalk in flip flops, yelling at the cars on the other side of the road to move, for God's sake, pull over so the dog doesn't get killed. The Great Dane stamped down the street like the Clydesdales in the Budweiser commercials and turned on Montana Avenue, heading toward the intersection of Bundy and

San Vincente: an overcrowded boulevard packed with cars. If the dog made it that far, there was no way that it would survive the four lanes of traffic, and if by some miracle it did, then I knew there was no way the dog would make it past Wilshire Boulevard a half mile down.

"Is that your dog?" a voice said.

When I turned around, there was a young woman in a brown Toyota sedan. She was wearing a winter hat, even though it wasn't cold.

"No," I said. "It's not your dog?"

She shook her head no. "I've been following the dog since Sunset." She meant Sunset Boulevard, but I pictured her chasing the dog as the sun raced across the sky, traversing the entire city like she was taking part in an ancient journey.

"You want to get in?" she asked.

I looked at the door handle and could see the dog further down Montana Avenue, forcing the cars in oncoming traffic to swerve out of the way. Without thinking, I felt my hand on the door handle and opened it, and on a random Sunday afternoon on a walk to grab coffee for my wife, I was suddenly in a car with a strange woman wearing a winter cap and trying not to smile when I sat in the car, and we were off, in search of a runaway dog.

"You see where he went?" she asked.

"I saw him head toward Whole Foods," I said.

She pulled off the curb and into traffic, and I stuck my head out of the window to flag down the attention of people walking. "Have you seen a dog?" I asked.

An older woman who looked startled when I called to her, simply pointed down the street to the alley behind Whole Foods, and the car swung into the alley with such speed and reckless abandon I wondered if people would think we were filming a chase scene in a movie. I looked through the parking lot and could see the dog in the middle of San Vincente, the leash dragging behind him, running with the traffic like he thought the aluminum cars were his pack.

"He's over there," I said.

She drove through the parking lot, passing the men in orange vests who needed to help the people in Brentwood back into their parking spaces like they didn't already have back-up cameras. She turned right on San Vincente, passing the bouquets of flowers on the side of Whole Foods, and we immediately hit a red light. Unlike the movies with great chase scenes, she didn't try and run the light. The line of traffic from Bundy was moving constantly through the street like a series of blood cells in a vein.

So we sat there in her car. She broke the silence first.

"You live around here?" she asked, the turn signal clicking in the silence.

"Just on Barrington," I said, sneaking a glance at her. She was my age, and I could tell she was smiling from the sides of her lips, almost like Mona Lisa: a smile that was implied rather than explicit. "Right near where you picked me up."

The turn signal clicked. It's hard to describe that silence. I could tell she wanted me to talk to her, but I felt held back, understanding that certain conversations are left better unexplored. When the light turned red, we spent the rest of the drive questioning where the dog had gone. *Do you think he turned off Bundy? Is it possible he circled back? Do you think his owner already found him?*

But as we drove further, it was clear that neither of us knew where the dog had gone. It had disappeared. I mentioned we should ask the people walking in the street if they saw a dog running. The first person we asked, a man who looked like he had been working in someone's garden—his hands and face and jeans were covered in dirt—pointed further down the road. The young woman with the skull cap looked at me and smiled, as if to say there was still hope.

She drove further down Bundy, passing Nicole Brown Simpson's old house, and we saw someone else in the street but no dog. This time it was an older woman in a walker and a younger man with black shades. The young man was holding the old woman by the arm.

"Have you seen a dog?" I asked.

"Is it your dog?"

"No."

"It was just running down the street," the old woman said. "It went that way. Toward Wilshire."

If the canine made its way to Wilshire without stopping, then there was no doubt that the animal had succumbed to a brutal death. Nothing could cross that road that was as wild and free as that dog. We kept on driving, closer and closer to the noisy intersection that spelled doom for the K-9, and the young woman stopped the car again. I asked a bystander, and they hadn't seen the dog. The trail was cold. We stopped and asked another person. But still, nothing.

We gradually crawled closer to Wilshire, and I stared at the constant traffic and listened to the engines and the honking like I was staring into a meat grinder. I asked the young woman to turn the car around, and she drove me back on Barrington Ave and dropped me in front of my apartment that looked like a motel, and I left without asking for her name.

Kare Kare

An Annotated Recipe[1]

THIS TRADITIONAL PILIPINO DISH IS A peanut butter oxtail stew served with eggplant, bok choy and string beans. Recipe yields one family-sized portion.

INGREDIENTS

2 ½ pounds oxtail[2]

¾ cup Jif peanut butter

5 Asian eggplant, sliced

1 fistful sitaw[3], green beans, cut into 2 -inch slices

3 pieces pechay, bok choy

1 packet kare kare seasoning

1 onion, chopped

2 cloves garlic, minced

Achuete oil

Salt and pepper

6 cups jasmine rice[4], cooked

Bagoong[5] shrimp paste

DIRECTIONS

1. Season oxtail with salt[6] and pepper, and add to 6 cups boiling water. Slow cook meat at least 2 hours or until tender. Skim off fat and set meat aside, saving broth in pot.

2. In separate pan, sauté onion and garlic. Combine with 1 cup oxtail broth, kare kare seasoning packet[7], and peanut butter.

3. In large pot, cook eggplant and sitaw in remaining broth. Add oxtail and peanut butter stew base. Simmer until stew thickens.
4. Stir in achuete until desired coloring is achieved. Add pechay and cover. Serve with jasmine rice and bagoong.

■ ■ ■

[1] The "uncle" my parents hired to serve food at Lola's funeral reception was an old family friend who once owed my grandmother money. I understood by the way he hurried to refill chafing dishes that he felt both sorry for our loss and thankful for the work. His heavy voice and distended belly, so at odds with Lola's lyrical breath and stooped figure, filled me with distaste, and eventual resignation. This uncle's sweaty forehead, and the purple cloths draping the tables in our backyard, were for years, the two most indelible images I recalled from her interment.

[2] The kare kare appeared more brown than orange, tasted flavorless and thin like most everything I ate following her passing. The oxtail had settled to the bottom of the pot, congealing with the stew, as if left too long in a pressure cooker. This kare kare was at best a poor imitation, failing to celebrate my grandmother, the matriarch who had brought such flavor to our family. Afterwards, I longed to stir my fingers into peanut butter and shrimp paste, into purple-gray flavor like back home.

[3] In the spring, she sat at our kitchen table, preparing kare kare, whirls of steam rising from the pot of oxtail cooking at the stove. The eggplant cut, and the bok choy washed, she split the ends of sitaw, rivulets of water slipping down her arms, charting the course of her wrinkles. I joined her with a kiss. The long green beans snapped beneath our fingers, the sound not unlike the pop Lola's knees made when she stood. Later, we would play cards at this same table, the smell of meat and starchy rice drifting between aces and eights, hearts and spades.

[4] Cook rice, Lola ordered. I worked at the sink, over the quick but necessary ritual, careful to stifle my huffs into sighs—as the youngest daughter it was my responsibility to make rice, never my brothers. My cupped palm worked as a sieve against the lip of the bowl, catching the grains and draining rice water. I rinsed the rice again and again, but not so many times that I washed away the flavor. Cup upon cup of rice, I have measured my life in rice cups.

[5] We ladled the kare kare over rice, pulling meat from the bone with a spoon and fork. I refused to eat it with the bagoong Lola offered. I could think of nothing less appetizing than purple-gray shrimp paste in a jar, except, of course, for dinuguan, the pig's blood dish we tried to feed our white friends, under the misnomer "chocolate soup." You don't know how to eat, Lola smiled around a spoonful. It was true, I ate more like an American than a Filipino, was more partial to cheeseburgers and pizza than to adobo and pancit.

[6] After the reception, we grandchildren sat in the living room, the fists on our knees still salty with grief. My mother divided the jewelry amongst us—rings, necklaces, charms—I watched these pieces of my grandmother disappear into siblings' hands, all the time dreaming of one more card game, one more kiss, one more spoonful, maybe this time, with bagoong.

[7] All those peculiar somethings, absent from the international aisle of my local grocery store, I found at the Ranch 99 Asian market. There, at last, were the foodstuffs of my childhood pantry: chicharon pork rinds, bottles of Mang Tomas and Jufran, longanisa sausage, cellophane-wrapped fish with crumbling tails, the crispy sesame sticks we dipped in chocolate, and blood red oxtail that begged to be slow cooked until scum floated to the surface of the water. There were the pink and yellow plastic bags of take-out containers with steam misshapen lids, purchased from Lola's mahjong winnings. The smell was one of many Saturdays. I stood in the seasonings

aisle, hoping to find my grandmother in a packet of spices and dust. She, who could make kare kare from scratch, used achuete seeds to color the stew a more delicious red orange—any attempts to recreate her cooking would doubtless fail. I could not reincarnate her kare kare, could not boil orange heart into a pot.

Translations

ANNA AKHMATOVA

TRANSLATED FROM RUSSIAN BY KATIE FARRIS AND ILYA KAMINSKY

Last Toast

I drink to our ruined house
To the evil of my life
To our loneliness together
And I drink to you—
To the lying lips that have betrayed us,
To the dead-cold eyes,
To the fact that the world is brutal and coarse
To the fact that God did not save us.

POLINA BARSKOVA

TRANSLATED FROM RUSSIAN BY KATIE FARRIS AND ILYA KAMINSKY

Two Poems

From Mad Vatslav's Diary

I was a coal-miner, water

Poured over my gray hair, my eyelashes.
My sister, alive and laughing,
Shepherded such glorious cows!

I was a soldier, and afraid of living
I did my best to die—but did not manage to stumble
Upon any bad luck. The tsar's own daughter
Visited my cabin and gave me a magic rope.

I was a slave. My master's wife
Adored us, the dark, forbidden Slavs.
The green sunrise was the strangest.
In sorrow I danced, swaying, trembling, on wooden porches.

Manuscript Found by Natasha Rostova During the Fire

I will try to live on earth without you.

I will try to live on earth without you.

I will become any object,
I don't care what—
I will be this speeding train.
This smoke
or a beautiful gay man laughing in the front seat.

A human body is defenseless
on earth.

It's a piece of fire-wood.
Ocean water hits it.
Lenin puts it on his official shoulder.

And therefore, in order not to suffer, a human spirit
lives
inside the wind and inside the wood and inside the should of a great
dictator.

But I will not be water. I will not be fire.

I will be an eyelash.
A sponge washing your neck-hairs.
Or a verb, an adjective, I will become. Such a word

slightly lights your cheek.
What happened? Nothing.
Something visited? Nothing.

What was there you cannot whisper.
No smoke without fire, they whisper.
I will be a handful of smoke
over this lost city of Moscow.

I will console any man,
I will sleep with any man,
under the army's traveling horse carriages.

JUSTYNA BARGIELSKA

TRANSLATED FROM POLISH BY MARIA JASTRZĘBSKA

Three Poems

In time for the gangway to close

So the weekend's over and I'm looking for your body
because it must be found and buried
and it will be my great joy if it's me
who is allowed to bury it, although can you speak of joy
when I know your body

ought to be in the desert being eaten by animals
till it vanishes? The same ought to happen
to my body when it finds yours
and sits down beside it.

To weep over your body, be eaten in my own,
to watch so that no one comes near is the challenge
I need to undertake so that someone, some time, understands
something of what happened here.

Two Fiats

I'm turning up the volume so The Lord will take me unto himself.
A man, a boy really with a white baby bath under his arm

and the lights of a small aeroplane on a distant runway
herald the same thing. A flower in black tulle on the seller's lapel,
the leaf which turned its silver underside to me
heralding the death of the heralded no matter
whether I rap them in cotton or foil.
We had children, but they weren't children, they were day shoes.
I'm not leaving you, shoes, I'm merely walking ahead.

Translation

From the street through the window I see my mum standing at the sink
in a burning house. I've been burning for a good while myself.
Not much is left of her, just her profile really. Thirty years will pass
and my daughter will watch me through a street window
burning in a burning house. I don't even know
if by then she'll know what she's watching.

I've made room for death in my life.
I've lifted off the quilt, my shirt, opened the rib cage.
I wouldn't have room for any of you if I hadn't made
room for death. Until I made room for death
I didn't have room for any of you, don't delude yourselves.
I crack open a walnut and find the ashes of a mouse,
husband and children, my prize, my confirmation.

ANNA AUGUSTYNIAK

TRANSLATED FROM POLISH BY DANUSIA STOK

I Loved, When She Departed

LOVED HIM, I LOOKED AT MY mother. Did she understand? She didn't turn her head, didn't lift her eyelids. She was going through something. I loved him, I tried a second time. He loved me too, you know? No response, mother was busy dying. When someone is busy dying, they don't have time for other things. Now I know. Then, it seemed there was still time for everything. Talk to her, pounded in my head. Do you remember how much he meant to me? You were with me right from the start, from the day I went to see him. I arrived an hour early. It was a good thing I wore that blue sheepskin. Snow crunched beneath my feet. I walked up and down in front of his house and when, at eight in the evening, I climbed the stairs, he shouted: One can set one's watch by you, you're so punctual. I had bought a sunflower with me. No idea why. It had these large, yellow petals. I found one on the stairs on my way out. It was like a spent tear. I didn't feel like crying. Maybe a little, with happiness. I returned in a taxi like Cinderella in a pumpkin carriage. Blurred streetlights in my eyes. They were my stars, which had suddenly sparkled when Amad kissed me. He sunk his tongue into me without a word. And I ran away. You know why, mum? My mother said something. Not to me. I took a risk: Really, mum? She confirmed. She was in some other world. They brought some fruit compote. I gave it to her, spoonful by spoonful, so she wouldn't choke. See how it smells of ripe sour cherries. She made a move, as though smelling it. She did it for me. Still demonstrating that she was with me. Not I with her, but she with me. She no longer opened her eyes but she didn't need to. We communicated more through murmurs anyway. Besides, she never opened her eyes again before dying.

A flower appeared on your skin, mum. A deathlike rose blossomed on the left side of your neck. As though you had had a tattoo. It was even pretty. We looked at it in detail, my sister and I. She touched it with her finger. Nobody else paid the rose any attention. Everybody was watching your lips, wanting you to smile. Wanting you to tell them that you were no longer in pain, that you felt better. They wanted to feel relief. That's why they had come, to be comforted. My sister wanted to hold on to you: If she could lie in the coffin like that, I'd visit her every day, caress her and do her hair. I've brought a brush and some hairspray. We started to comb your hair. It wasn't easy because your hair was dirty, someone had soaked it in something sticky. But my sister insisted. She combed your fringe, put stray locks behind your ears then released them, while I sprayed lacquer from a distance. Cover her eyes, I said and immediately it flashed through my mind that lacquer doesn't sting the eyes of those who are dead. But my sister held both hands tightly over your eyes.

I dreamt of you again. Ever since you died, you've been with me every night. Maybe I'm the one who's not letting you go?

She was my whole life, said my sister. Now I no longer have anything. You have everything, Amad used to say to me, you've got me. I was radiant then, although I didn't really have anything. All that was mine were words. I liked them, constantly hungered for them.

I'm coming to see you. What kind of you? My father says that it's raining again and everything's falling on you. What does that matter, I reply with feigned indifference. What does it matter to you, mum? I didn't protect you. Allowed all this. I didn't scream, there were no tears. A trumpet was playing while I stared at the surrounding hundred-year-old oaks and pine forest. The call of birds filled the space between branches. Somehow it was so dense despite the young leaves. The sun shone through. Fine and pleasant. Shall I tell you all this, or do you already know? Bethey lowered the coffin into the grave, I looked to see what awaited you. A hiding place, as for an animal or Jew. A hollow, lined with concrete. It's now that we have to hide you? But you're beautiful. Father boasted that, wherever you went, you stood out. They say that about me, too, although I am only a little like you. Bold and abrasive. I have your amazing legs and long, black hair. Except you styled yours like Brigitte Bardot or, maybe, Sophia Loren, I don't know anymore. I can imagine you poring over their photographs. What could you know about the world then. You cut photographs out and stuck them down between recipes for deep-fried biscuits and sponge cakes. You dragged the huge notebook with you all your life, from house to house. The yellowed pages are crumbling, the stains left by greasy fingers have smudged your lettering, but Bardot with her full hips still poses sexily for what must now be half a century. My mother between black covers of thick cardboard. I did not want to be like you at all; into my scrapbooks I stuck stories about African animals.

I watched you gasping for air. You needed oxygen. No, it's better not to give her any otherwise she won't die, I thought. And death was already lying in wait. The one from Beksiński's painting. I used to dream of having it up on my wall. Now it has crawled under your bed. Kneeling in front of you, eyes bound in a bloodied bandage. It's going to take you away from me, I know that, I just don't know when. Yet, in spite of that, I want to stroke it. Not so as to tame it, simply as a gesture of gratitude for standing over you, too. See, mummy dear, you can keep dying as long as you like. Barely panting, but not alone. Well, without oxygen because why go on promising you life, why connect you to the world. Free, you were passing away completely free.

Do spirits of the deceased respond to cries for help? Mum! Mum! It is not true that you're not here. You cannot not be, after all you have always been. You are my beginning. I cannot go any further without your eyes holding me. No-one else but Amad could look at me like that. He would light a cigarette and sink his eyes into me. I blew at the smoke but he grimaced and muttered: Stop it, nothing's going to happen to you. He scrutinized me. I loved the way he looked at me. I squirmed like a little girl, tensed like a woman. He was evaluating me. I would have done anything to get top marks. I even stopped breathing. I was a sculpture which never lowers its eyes. Waiting for Amad to turn away.

There are traces of hands in my garden. You stroked the euonymus and laughed when I didn't let you prune the branches. But shrubs like it, you said and formed ball after ball from boxwood. They grew back unevenly; they waited for you in autumn. You didn't come. They continued waiting after winter. Spring passed. The magnolias didn't blossom. The roses overgrew with thorns. The crown imperials bowed their empty chalices. Where is mother, who nurtured the catkins on the willows and the Himalayan wallichiana pinus tree with its long, soft needles faintly coated in wax? Now its skin is covered with a layer of wax as though stopping what remained of life from evaporating. Where is mother, now it is I who ask. She's dead, go and fetch somebody, says my sister. Who? Whoever. Excuse me madame, I think my mother has just died.

I always had a few pills of morphine in my jeans. In the event of sudden pain, I could quickly give you one. But you weren't very willing. You wriggled out of swallowing your next dose. I have to see how much my system can take, you repeated, one shouldn't give up so easily, pain has to be controlled. Does control mean suffering, curling up in spasms and screaming into the pillow? Why are you doing this, I asked. Go away, you said.

Her eyes. With black patches on the irises. Green or hazelnut? I have to recall their hue. It's hard, which is why I search for it in photographs. Is it possible that their colour could alter so much? As though each photographer gave them his own tone. Or maybe it was clothes that changed her eyes. They grew lighter when she wore beiges or creams. Filled with warmth next to browns. But when she drank cognac, they dulled. No, first fear disappeared so that mother's eyes began to sparkle. Only later, when the bottle was nearly empty, did they dull. For me, she died at those moments. She would stand the last glass of cognac by her bed. Usually, the little glass just stood there and stood, while she slept. She never drank stale alcohol later. Besides, she had a rule: the following day she would refuse whatever the occasion. No, thank you, I always heard. I would run after her with the bottle; she would turn her head away with repulsion. She would look at me as at a child who, without understanding, was playing with adult objects. And she took offence at being photographed with a glass in hand. I used to do it on purpose, waiting for the moment when she would part her lips, pour the cognac down and grimace. That's what I was looking for. But you don't like the taste, I would say, so why drink? Just like your father, you replied, you don't even know how to have fun.

God, who hath created heaven and earth and deceived me, death is not life. Since my mother died forever, amen, I no longer believe you. I don't give a shit for the rewards of martyrdom and for meat which is raised from the dead. I want my worldly mother.

You said you heard music. What's happening to my head, you asked. I wanted to pretend that I heard it too, but I couldn't. I, who had almost become an actress. Come closer, girl, let your hair down. She looks more feminine straightaway, doesn't she, rector? "Apart—but one remembers the other, Between us flies the white dove of sorrow Continually carrying news . . ." No, it doesn't go like that, said Amad, listen: "In every place, and at each time of day, Where once we played, or where once we had wept, Everywhere, ever, with you I shall stay—There, then, a part of my soul I had left." And he was with me. And you were always there where he was, with me.

Your body was fermenting, while I prayed to God, the three-in-one. Once, I spoke to him all night. I wanted to hear: I am here who am. I wanted to hear: I will be here with you who will be here with you. Yahweh, I needed neither manna nor quails. I sought a power which would open my mother's stomach. Who was I then that I spoke your name with mortal lips? Until you said: Still your pain, daughter. You were the God of my father, I listened to you.

Or else you'll become a hunter, you laughed at me. Miss hunter, Amad called me. Yes, I wanted to dig something up from my head. From the fantasies with which I lived. Miss fantasist.

Has the cancer gone there with you? The son-of-a-whore.

The brain is short of oxygen, the lady doctor said, the convulsions have already started. I never imagined it to be like this. In films, dying is always dignified. One can cry and hold out a hand in farewell. Your hands were wrung by the convulsions. You flung yourself around on the bed. Mum, you don't have to get up, lie down a little longer, I said. With difficulty, you lay down again. Apparently your ethereal body was retreating from you. You can see it in the eyes, but yours were closed all the time. I looked around at the walls. Maybe those little holes were scraped out by others who were dying? Didn't they believe that they'd penetrate the wall anyway? I touched your fingers. They were only a little older than mine. I remember how you used to keep injuring them when washing glasses.

But what if she's not dead? She's definitely dead, said my sister. She hasn't moved since Saturday. It's only the third day, I thought. I knew she wasn't playing with us at pretending. She wouldn't know how to act in a comedy. She is lying motionless, as though the end of the world has come. For mother's body, this was the end of the world. She had crossed death into a new life. What life, she's lying there like a log. I'm cold, mum. I'm kneeling on the floor. Get up, your knees will catch cold. It's best you sit down. I'm cold. It has to be cold for mum and the others. Don't be frightened of her, I hear father's voice, you don't have to touch her at all if you don't want to. I wouldn't touch her for the life of me. So you are afraid. No, I'm just disgusted. Ah, yes.

She's ready. She's got gold rings on her fingers. In her right-hand pocket, a medallion woven from silver thread. Inside are miniature photographs. Three little heads. We will be with you wherever you go. We won't leave you alone, I think. I lower my eyes as the lid covers your face. I don't try to cram anything into the coffin. It might seem I'm made of stone. But I'm made from her, from her body. Even our bellies are identical. And that similar absence of shame. It comes from indifference. Anybody can touch us.

The coffin stands in the middle. You are lying with your back to the angels in the picture. Where are you, mum. It's good she's not suffering anymore, somebody says. There, look how she's smiling. I get up and see that you're smiling. You've betrayed me. Our serial was never supposed to come to an end.

She is looking at monkeys again, my father is furious. If the monkeys are there when I come in the morning, you won't get any breakfast, says my sister, give yourself a break, at least over the weekends. Illusory monkeys which menstruate every four weeks. Rhesuses with strong facial muscles and complicated facial expressions, which recognize their reflection in the mirror. What were you looking for in their world, mum? The same as was in yours? Infantine swamp monkeys. You took care of us possessively. The course in life lessons was not wasted. We are strong and very well trained. You even gave us freedom but made sure we did not leave your body. You had two embryos to the very end.

You are in a new reality. So what's it like there, mum, with no bad spirits? At the beginning of Mass, along with the angels and heavenly hosts everybody sang, asking God to absolve you of sins. What sins, I thought and pretended to sing. You're pure, transparent. Before you died, a Eucharistic minister came with the oleum infirmorum. I didn't know how to behave, should I leave the oil on your forehead? Because you immediately wiped it off your hands. I was scared of touching it with a handkerchief, cleansing away its healing power. This was already the second time you were anointed. I thought it was a sin. Maybe that's good, you would have something to your name, some little matters, prisoner of the body. You sin in thought, another priest said one day, sitting in your armchair, but he absolved the thoughts. You remember? He was talking about the sacrament in which God brushes against a person's skin. Timidly. The touch had to be tender because you were so clearly suffering. I wanted a sign that you'd felt the finger of God. But nothing happened. Only pain. Your consecrated pain. You lay like an effigy in van der Weyden's painting. I looked for the scene a long time. The figures in their enchanted positions. Like us. A game played out between the living. You on the threshold of something. I in silent dread of it taking place. "Through this holy anointing may the Lord in His love and mercy help you with the grace of the Holy Spirit. May the Lord who frees you from sin save you and raise you up. Amen." Amen, I said.

You wandered through Nałkowska's rooms, looked out of the window: Here's where yuccas could flower. You dug some out of your garden and brought them. Leaves like the swords of palm in rosette form. Flowers on a three-metre long pole. A plume of cream-coloured bells. The flowerbeds soaked up the sweet aroma. It was as a complete woman ought to be. And only the head satiated with after-images. My head and yours. Who did you love most? What do you mean who? My husband. Mother gazes at her reflection in the mirror. Clumsily, she tries to tidy her hair. She assures me and herself: My husband, of course. Tomorrow she will already be dead. She is still so beautiful that she could lie in a coffin with a glass lid. All the more so as she will be wearing her cream blouse and pearl-buttoned cardigan. Father says to dress her in her black or navy-blue suit. Like Aunty Dotty, I think. Like they dressed Nałka. But she was about seventy, who would dress her in a polka-dot frock? She's got to have what she liked, says my sister, and we start to take knickers, bras and tights out of the wardrobe. Not black at all. I watch my sister lay everything out on the bed. As though packing mother's bag for a holiday. There won't be any more holidays. A long dying of summer. Withered trees. That's what lies ahead of us. You didn't like autumn. But I do. I used to wallow in leaves up to my ankles. Closed my eyes in rapture. The rustle, crunch, decay. Is that why you raked the lawns around Nałkowska's house? I did it so as to be close to literature, I was fifteen. You nod, amused. The other I from the house on the meadows senses within herself the ability to reject all dogma. Later, I will also turn away from God. Because of Amad, the first man in my life. But I'll refuse when he wants me to conceive his child so as to pass original sin on to it.

They cut your breast off, like St Barbara's. Apparently God is very greedy for pain. Apparently pain is punishment for sin. What did you have to be punished for? Saint Amazon. Celestial better half. Proud woman, look around. See? You liked to come here. Once a year, they opened the wooden gates to the three Renaissance altars of St Barbara. You keep a photograph of the larch sanctuary in a casket. The presbytery facing east. That is where Christ is to appear from. You were already waiting for his second coming then. So don't be surprised that persecutions had to be suffered in his name. I remember how you showed me the sentenced breast. It was January. And how, without a word of complaint, you showed me the place where the full breast with its pinkish nipple had once been. In February. Did Christ take your misery upon himself? Or was it you who, attenuating for the sins of the world, carried his cross? You were half resurrected with a pearl coloured scar which changed colours when the sun fell on it. And with every year that passed, it kept on shrinking. You said: Look, it's disappearing, merging into the skin as though it was trying to erase any trace of what used to be there. Mother, flat as a boy. And you, enchanting Barbara, whose breast was torn out with iron talons. Succour of the dying. Patron of the graveyard. I call you as the tempest rages within me. I peer into the eye sockets of your skull. Closed within the reliquary as in a crown. And my mother's head imprisoned in a coffin of knarled wood.

We laughed when you got words wrong. You gazed at the dusty cabinet and said: Everything's covered in cream. Or: We've got to go and beg in the shop. You observed us carefully as we fell about laughing. It was the same when we were children; a wiggle of the finger was enough for us to make each other giggle as though wound up. Gigglers, you called us then. When sounds terrified you, we called the doctor. We need to increase the steroids. So we did. Look, we still want to laugh. You've died, and we can still laugh.

I couldn't tell you about my best lover. I didn't have the courage. Only in my dreams did I confess to you that Amad took me from the back. This is what happened. We were going to Lavender for lunch. He turned on the stairs and shouted: How beautiful you are! God, how I fancy you, I've got to screw you. He caught me by the hand and pulled me into the apartment. I gave in. Besides I was excited, because, in Lavender, he was going to tell me whether I was going to become his wife. He needed three days to think it over. Later, we ate fish and the sun was shining. In the evening, I called to tell you all about it. As usual, I couldn't.

Your red hair is sparkling on the brush. That's how it'll stay. What was it like to the touch? I can't remember. I washed and combed it before you died, but I've forgotten everything. Even your Boo Boo fringe, as my sister and I called it when you used to come back from the hairdresser. About your skin, I know everything. What it was like. Well, no, I didn't touch you needlessly. You didn't like that. After all, there was no question of any familiarity. Even in kissing you would offer one cheek then the other, as in the Bible. Your entire last day, I coated your lips with lipstick as though I'd gone mad. Premortal fever burned your lips. I painted and you puffed out your lips, created bumps and waves. You pouted. I could see that it made you laugh, making you beautiful like that. Normally, if you had been able to speak, you certainly wouldn't have concealed your irritation. You kept losing consciousness; that protected me. Maybe I even stroked your hair. I'm trying to find some memories. But there is no image within me. As though I had never laid my hands on your head. Only once you had died did I nestle into your neck and kiss your hair, wind it around my fingers and whisper in your ear: Mum, mum.

FABIO MORÁBITO

TRANSLATED FROM SPANISH BY CURTIS BAUER

Three Prose Pieces

To Transcend the Face

I often run around a track and, when I approach it, I am still too far away to distinguish the runners by their faces, but I can recognize them by the way they run, which is unmistakable, and over time this is how I've become familiar with each one. Our ability to recognize subjects by the way they run is the same that allows us to become intimate with a character in a novel. In nineteenth-century century novels authors felt compelled to give an exhaustive description of every character, from the color of her hair and eyes, even his clothing. They took a photo of them, literally. But it was a useless photo since the characters acquired a face through their actions and words, a subjective and different face for every reader, a memorable, unphotographable face. The modern novel assimilated this lesson and now we know that the reader doesn't need to attach a face to the characters. They relate to them through low-frequency waves, such as those used by elephants to communicate over great distances. These waves have a long reach because they skip over the faces, which are a secondary detail, and they adjust to/bend around what is most meaningful which, in the case of the elephant, can be the size of another herd, its location and the direction it moves. For both us and elephants, the low frequency sacrifices the face to inform us about the behavior of the other, which allows us to recognize a body from a distance without going into details, and one of the reasons that we are disappointed with a movie when we compare it to the novel that inspired it is that it shows us the faces of the characters, which we had been saved from by reading the book. That is why good actors are those who carry us toward that singular and unphotographable face, which is behind the outward face, and the art of the novel, in a similar manner, is the art of transcending the face, transporting us to the submerged and unique dimension of our behavior, to our deep style, where there are no masks.

Kafka and Names

Kafka's best stories always begin with a name: "As Gregor Samsa awoke one morning . . ."; "someone must have been telling lies about Josef K."; "it was already dark when K. came to the village." Kafka clings to a name as a castaway to a plank. He never retreats from this stronghold. Once he's found a protagonist he doesn't let him go for a second and as the story unfolds he harvests new names reluctantly, bound by the mechanics of the story; if it were up to him he would keep only one character, with only one name, and this name would be reduced to only one letter and that letter would always be the same, the emblematic K. of his own last name. He has an aversion to proper names because they tear the fabric of the narrative, which he conceives as a continuous secretion; you only need to look at how infrequently he uses new paragraphs; he is the writer of new sentences; his prose pattern is a murmur in continuous expansion; he chooses to name at the beginning of the story when the reader is unprepared and can withstand this bitter pill, but once that story has weighed anchor he is careful to name as little as possible. He was one of the few to be conscious of the anomaly of proper names, those words which specify a single individual and are therefore a kind of language black hole. Let us not forget that he was bookkeeper in an insurance company. His meticulously uniform style has the neatness of account books. He dreamed perhaps of writing a book without anything shocking, methodically sequential like a ledger. In his diary he confessed: "When writing a story I don't have the time, which would be necessary, to expand in all directions." It is what a spider desires: to weave a fabric of endless associations, without leaving a single space uncovered. Therefore he avoids proper names, which, through their innocence, ease linguistic tension and form openings, magical gaps. And they also form, in the peaceful relaxation of writing, impenetrable castles. Everything that a proper name possesses within itself and there is no way to argue with that!

Dostoevsky

Reading Dostoevsky reminds us that human life is, first and foremost, dialogue. None of his characters are word deprived. As soon as the name of a character is mentioned, the story seems committed to lead us, no matter how many twists and turns may be required to do this, to hear his voice, because only a voice grants his characters a statute of reality. It is important that when Dostoevsky feels obliged to narrate a series of events which we need to understand the story, he does so like someone opening a parenthesis. He often calls these sections "summaries" and seems to apologize to the reader for having to use them. He treats them like foreign bodies and as soon as he can he goes back to his dialogues, which are the true developers of the plot. The characters' thoughts are dialogic, intimate disputes that each have with themselves. Dostoevsky would never have been able to write the story of Robinson Crusoe. He would have thought it was a waste of time to tell us how a castaway manages to convert his island into a comfortable home. Ultimately Robinson Crusoe shows us that it is possible to live without any dialogue. For Dostoyevsky the human being is a castaway, but a castaway in the midst of other castaways, each one on an island he will never be able to leave. Today we find his dialogues extravagant and the power that sustains them, which is the attraction each character feels toward the other, seems incomprehensible. Our fellow human no longer awakens our curiosity. We are dedicated to making our small island more and more comfortable. These impulsive and infantile characters seem ridiculous, and the ridiculous is a constant in the stories of this Russian writer, the ridiculous that is always an excess of curiosity, of expansion, of surrender and interference, contrary to Robinson Crusoe, whose saga can be seen as the most complete victory over ridiculousness, the triumph of a man who has removed all surprise and excesses from his surroundings.

ANJA (KAURANEN) SNELLMAN

TRANSLATED FROM FINNISH BY MAIJA MÄKINEN

Excerpt of *Pelon maantiede* ("Geography of Fear")

THERE WAS A GAME WE USED to play on Sheep Island, at the Camp.

I call it a game now. The whole Geography of Fear seminar seemed, especially in the beginning, like a fanatical pastime for grownups, akin to the leadership training seminars with their retreats, or the latest staff-recruitment stratagem—a paint-ball battle in a suburban forest, a canoe expedition, or a wilderness tour in the northern mountains.

We were all sitting in the stone labyrinth, in the front yard of the House of Weary Women, eating mushrooms, drinking them, chewing them, climbing inside our chosen folktales, taking the human and animal forms we knew from Finnish folktales.

The first time, I grew a pair of long ears and twitchy feet. My nose began to quiver so briskly that my glasses fell to the ground.

I was a hare.

"Transmogrification—to animal, plant, or even mineral—must be the most radical of seductions?" Maaru said, her eyes burning.

"The shape-shifting makes us traitors to our own species, susceptible to the experience of another. It's like the seduction of love. In love, it's the strangeness of the other gender we seek, and the chance to be initiated into it as if to a different species of animal or plant. Seduction is the art of disappearing from the self!"

Once upon a time there was a Parson's Wife With No Shadow, whose name and fate both stemmed from the fact that she had no desire to bear children.

Once there was also a Soulless Shrew, whose name and fate came from the fact that she had bundled and drowned all twelve of her sons—she had not wanted to birth boys, only girls.

Maaru is talking, talking, talking.

She has her palms over my face. My eyes are open, and with her small pale hands there, it is as though I'm looking at an open book.

The book tears in two as she spreads her hands and bends down to kiss me on the mouth with her chapped, bleeding lips. She slides the tip of her tongue over the surface of my teeth. That's the part of the dream where I always wake up.

The Walkman has tumbled to the floor, the earphones have popped out of my ears. I hear the thin, distant voice of Kiri Te Kanawa singing *Ruhe, ruhe, meine Seele, und vergiss, was dich bedroht.*

Under the stonewashed sky, the field on our tiny island is so barren and cold, growing bulrush and sparse spikelets of oat—wild oat, ergot.

Maaru sings the words, they come out of her mouth.

Maaru and I, moments before our final supper, standing in the middle of Sheep Island's sole, marshy field (the turnip patch that, according to the Archive of Happiness, Alma Vartiainen tilled productively in 1909–1914 for an annual rent of 350 Finnish marks).

Darkness has fallen. Through the trees, the sea glints silver and grey, the waves welling away from the island like in the Tennyson poem my mother used to quote and that I never fully understood.

The soggy silt and black earth squelch under our feet. We are standing where the men lie; I know we are just about on top of them.

No woman has ever kissed me like that. Has anyone? It is like a brand or a mark, a direct blow and a coming apart at the same time. It could be a blow, but it is a kiss.

Maaru strikes me with her broken lips.

This is how it happens.

"Look," Maaru whispers and points at the sky with her finger. "The casual flick of God's wrist across the August sky.

"From the Equator to the Antarctic, He scatters the stars, flings them high enough so people don't slip over all that miasma." Maaru parts her lips and grimaces.

When I look up, craning my neck so that it crunches, Maaru grips my shoulders and without warning kisses me on the mouth, roughly. Our teeth clash and I immediately taste blood. Maaru's breasts butt against mine, and I touch her neck and feel soft skin and coarse stubble.

As she watches my face, Maaru says in a whisper that she has shocked many men by fucking them with her clitoris, "right inside that little orifice they have at the tip of their organ."

"Miniature sex," Maaru whispers hoarsely. "So you see, I've jammed other things in there besides knitting needles."

With that she bursts out laughing, her face twisting, sliding downward. She leans into me, her cheekbone against my collarbone; we are both so thin our bones are conversing.

The mushrooms flash in front of my eyes—flat convex shaped, bell shaped, conical, scaped, umbilicate, funnel shaped and flat—all the mushrooms we have consumed over the last several weeks. The urge to vomit rises, as always after our meals, and the violent convulsions knock me down as I struggle to overcome them. I don't want to reveal to her the shape I'm in; I don't want Maaru to see inside me.

As much as she knows about guts, she will never know the secret of mine.

Shaking, I try to focus on a single detail. Often it works. This time I fix my gaze on Maaru's neck and throat.

Her cameo pendant hangs from its smudged, yellowed velvet ribbon. "Glyptic art," Maaru has often said, "stone engraving—an undervalued field of research; these cameos were originally used as seals, customized for each individual."

Maaru's face close to mine; she's wiping the corners of her eyes with her arms and hands, like a child, her eye patch pulled up to her forehead like a hair band, the way she liked to wear it; her puckered mouth, her perpetually alert hazel eyes and black eyebrows, her dry lips, chapped to a dim grey; the resplendent scent of earth after rainfall, the efflorescence of stars in the sky, our muddy boots firmly in the boggy soil, in water that neither flows nor is replenished.

I knew that time was running out. We had no radio, read no papers, and none of the people who occasionally tramped through the island brought messages of any kind. Yet I could see it on Maaru that the end was near. She had been restless and keyed up for days, behaving much like a person in the acute throes of infatuation.

The time had come to pledge that other allegiance.

I sensed that Maaru was prepared to do almost anything that anyone thought to suggest; she stayed awake around the clock and roamed the island's shorelines, looking out toward the city. Sometimes, instead of sleeping in my reversible "bum's jacket," I wanted to lie down beside Maaru in her down sleeping bag, the way Johanna did; suddenly I realized I'd always wanted that. I wanted to sleep next to Maaru, my arm around her.

We never made a decision.

Or at least I never heard of one. To this day I cannot say for certain whether what happened to the women was only an accident.

Reviews

Portrait of the Poet as Critic (& Thinker)

Francisco Aragón

185

Portrait of the Poet as Critic (& Thinker)

"Doing what I set out to do, perform activism with ink."

—RIGOBERTO GONZÁLEZ

TWO FRIENDS ARE CHATTING OVER LUNCH in New York. One is a native of Texas, the other is from California. Both are Chicano authors. During dessert a cellphone rings. Texas takes the call. The brief consultation ends and Texas shifts his gaze back to California and says, "You want to review books?" This would have been 2002. And so . . . the poet Rigoberto González soon inaugurates his stint as a critic by reviewing *From the Other Side of Night* by Francisco X. Alarcón.

By the time it wound down ten years later, González's Latinx book column had achieved legendary status—with 206, I repeat, 206 reviews filed. He hadn't sought out this role. Ramón Rentería, the features editor at the *El Paso Times*, came calling—following up on fiction writer Sergio Troncoso's recommendation. An opportunity presented itself and González embraced it.

In essence, he taught himself how to write the book review, taking on the novel, short story, nonfiction and poetry collection alike. I remember him once remarking that the more of these he penned and published the more he internalized the genre of the 500-word review. González had perceived a glaring gap where the critical attention of Latinx books was concerned—and was determined to do something about it. These reviews laid the foundation for what became but one side of his multi-faceted vocation— that of activist critic.

That ethos is what drives *Pivotal Voices, Era of Transition: Towards a 21ˢᵗ Century Poetics* (University of Michigan Press, 2017), which gathers, in its three sections, "Critical Essays," "Critical Reviews" and "Critical Grace Notes." In a way, it's a companion to *Red-Inked Retablos* (University of Arizona Press, 2013), his first book of critical writing. But as much as I enjoyed that Arizona book (I'm thinking, in particular, of the essays on the late Andrés Montoya and the late Roxana Rivera, as well as "The Truman Capote Aria"), this volume's arc feels more realized and coherent.

I

Critical Essays

The book opens with a lecture ("Pivotal Voices, Era of Transition") delivered at the Library of Congress. González dedicates this talk to José Montoya—the late Chicano maestro and former poet laureate of Sacramento. This homage near the beginning provides a seamless transition to discuss Eduardo C. Corral's poem, "Variation on a Theme by José Montoya." Corral is the first of six poets González centers his remarks on. The others are J. Michael Martínez, David Tomás Martínez, Carmen Giménez Smith, Laurie Ann Guerrero, and Cynthia Cruz. This curated roster functions like a snapshot of Latinx poetry's aesthetic range—especially with the inclusion of Michael Martinez and Giménez Smith who, arguably, serve as stand-ins for *Angels of the Americlypse*, an anthology from that same year (2014) that highlights the more innovative tendencies in Latinx writing. The inclusion of Cynthia Cruz is welcome recognition that Latinx poets don't all write about identity, and that Latinx poets come from a range of ancestries as well, including German. Opening the book with a piece connected to our national library in Washington, D.C., also subtly affirms that the poems emerging from Latinx communities are essential to the literary conversations taking place across the United States.

In his Acknowledgements page at the very beginning of the book, González thanks Kazim Ali for his "persistence and patience," suggesting

Ali's editorial vision—as the Poets on Poetry series co-editor—planted the seed that became *Pivotal Voices*. González ends his brief preface to part one by remarking:

> [T]here is something absolutely marvelous in the knowledge that people like ourselves made the glorious decision to imagine our bodies, our bodies of color, our queer bodies of color, as empowered participants and protagonists—away from the edges of alienation and exile and closer to the truths of our unerasable realities.

Rigoberto González is insinuating, then, that one of his principal aims as a critic is to bolster the work of queer writers of color. Nearly half of the pieces in section one discuss Eduardo C. Corral, Danez Smith, Rajiv Mohabir, Ocean Vuong, and Natalie Diaz.

The piece on Mohabir and Vuong ("Queer Immigrant World, Queer Immigrant Word") is based on the *unpublished* manuscripts of what became their debut volumes of poetry, underscoring a desire to amplify *newer* voices of color. At the beginning of this illuminating essay, González mentions running into Vuong and Mohabir at local literary events, and being delighted to learn that their first books would be published in the same year, therefore "reach[ed] out to them for permission for an early glimpse of their works . . ." It's also personal: "I related to their immigrant upbringing and to their journey as artists."

And yet at the start of the aforementioned LOC lecture González comments on "the literary legacy of those who, long before many of us even knew how to read, placed expression on the page in order to inspire, motivate, and educate the audience of their time and the audience to come." Thus, the second "Critical Essay" is "Alurista: Towards a Chicano Poetics." What I found of particular interest here is that González reveals his own evolution of thought, where this Chicano elder is concerned: "For the longest time I, too, accepted these notions and helped circulate them whenever I was asked about Alurista." One of the notions he's referring to is that Alurista was an "experimental" poet. He persuasively argues why this is too tidy, perhaps too lazy a way of characterizing Alurista's work, and instead offers astute analysis of what he prefers to call his "wordplay" and "the way he configures many of his poems on the page," as well as his linguistic strategy of adopting "Spanish, English, Spanglish, Caló, and so on." Also useful is how he links Alurista to his junior high classmate in San Diego, Juan Felipe Herrera. As a former U.S. Poet Laureate, Herrera may, understandably, be more well-known than Alurista in mainstream poetry circles, and so linking the two will hopefully garner Alurista new readers.

But the pieces from this first section that most engaged me were the ones that highlighted single authors—specifically, the four studies on Eduardo C. Corral, Aracelis Girmay, Danez Smith, and Natalie Diaz, respectively. González varies his strategy when approaching each of these poets. With Aracelis Girmay, for example, he opens with a brief discussion of her Eritrean, Puerto Rican, and African American ancestry as a way of arguing for "a particular lens that textures the reading experience . . ." With Natalie Diaz, he contexualizes her among other high-profile native poets before diving into his examination of *When My Brother Was an Aztec*. But as introductions go, his opening remarks on Danez Smith felt the most timely and compelling—the way they address, on the one hand, the "alarming increase in cases across the country of racist profiling, police brutality, self-appointed vigilantism, and other prejudicial acts that have resulted in the deaths of young black men . . ." and, on the other hand, offer a brief roll call of African American poets who have, in their own way, responded to these tragic outcomes. In short, he provides a rich political and poetic context before situating Smith's work within it. González excels at providing just the right proportion of poetic citations (not too many) and snippets of engaging analysis (a larger dose)—so much so it enticed this reader to seek out the book under discussion, *[insert] boy*. Here's how González unpacks that single word ("boy"):

In its racial context it gestures to its use as an infantilizing address, from a white man to black man, that expresses both condescension and derision. In gay parlance it is a designation given to a younger man, typically a youth, but in relationship dynamics a "boy" is a willing object of desire of an older male, sometimes referred to as 'daddy'. Therein the intriguing tension in the word...

In discussing a poem from the final section of the book, González skillfully weaves commentary with citation to provocative effect:

And in 'Cue the Gangsta Rap When My Knees Bend,' the speaker is being ironic in his own fetishizing of the 'thug' image, fulfilling his own sexual fantasy: 'The only word my mouth cares for is O'

And yet, in considering this quartet of reviews, something surprising occurred. The piece on the poet whose work I was *most* acquainted with ended up being the piece that most spoke to me. You see, I went in with the faulty and false assumption that "The Twenty-First-Century Queer Chicano Poetics of Eduardo C. Corral" would be the essay I'd learn the *least* from. Instead, something resembling the opposite unfolded.

For the last several years now, ekphrastic poetry—poetry inspired by art—has been a particular interest of mine, both as a poet and as a literary curator, and so I found myself enthralled with the beginning of González's discussion of *Slow Lightning*—through this particular lens:

The painting in question shows a fawn-like figure wearing a crown of flowers, eyes like a cat's, devouring a bird. The physical act is the satiating of both bodily hunger and sexual appetite. The fluidity of this animal-human relationship gestures toward the transformation of Greek myth and to the Amerindian indigenous animal spirits or *nahualismo*—the animal soul manifested in dream, story, and art. Another name for this fluidity of influences and dialogues is borderlessness.

González, in effect, is enacting what he's about to discuss—Corral's ekphrastic poem. He's become, in this snippet of prose, an ekphrastic critic.

Growing up, as I did, in a bilingual household; majoring in Spanish literature in college; living in Spain for a decade; publishing a completely dual-language book of poems—that is, because of all of these things, it was inevitable that a poetics like Corral's, one which deploys more than one tongue, would inherently interest me. And so, when it came time for González to broach this strand of Corral's poetics, I'm happy to report that I wasn't disappointed. On the contrary:

> The use of multiple languages can be unsettling, but the purpose is not to leave the reader with a feeling of alienation after this encounter; rather, Corral invites the reader to enter the territory of the borderlands, where such linguistic auditory experiences are commonplace.

Drawing a parallel between a page of intralingual poetry and a swath of the borderlands—the space between the U.S. and Mexico—really leapt off the page for me!

While carefully re-reading the essay the text morphed into a plaza for the three of us:

> queer son-of-immigrants subject (Corral)
> queer son-of-immigrants critic (González)
> queer son-of-immigrants reader (Aragón)

This configuration unfurled as I marveled, was moved by, González's multi-pronged treatment of the speaker's father. I love this passage:

> In a sense, in order to claim full agency of his sexuality, the son needs to leave the father and find possibility outside of his childhood home, even if it is just next door. Unburdened by social or religious pressures,

the speaker is free to dream, desire, and imagine. Perhaps the lines of the poem "Saint Anthony's Church" say it best: 'Instead of the nailed palms of Christ, / my father's warm hand on my shoulder.'

Two of Corral's poems also don the same "haunting title": "Acquired Immune Deficiency Syndrome." González aptly characterizes Corral's approach to these as "more elliptical," but doesn't shy away from taking them on while acknowledging that they "leave much room for interpretation." With one of the poems, he argues that it's "futile to impose definition" on an elegant, image-rich, micro-surreal narrative. Instead, these poems are "conceptual pieces, the antithesis of death, decay, and darkness." They are "acts of vibrancy, song, and light." I especially appreciated these readings because they are in sync with what I often say to my students—that poems, like songs whose lyrics we may not fully comprehend, can still be enjoyed for the sounds they make—the sounds that pass through our bodies.

II

Critical Reviews

Even though section two of the book clocks in with three *fewer* pieces than section one, it engages the work of twenty-four poets. But one of its pieces accounts for half this number: "Twelve Essential Latino Poetry Books." Rigoberto González has made a selection from his *El Paso Times* reviews and placed them under this "umbrella" title. He has often said that poetry is his first love. Therefore, I'd venture a guess that half of his 200+ EPT reviews were on books of poetry. This means that he may very well have curated these twelve poetry book reviews from, roughly, one hundred poetry book reviews. Here they are, in the order they appeared:

Francisco X. Alarcón's *From The Other Side of Night* (University of Arizona Press, 2002)
Brenda Cárdenas' *Boomerang* (Bilingual Press, 2010)

Blas Manuel De Luna's *Bent to the Earth* (Carnegie Mellon University Press, 2005)

David Dominguez's *Work Done Right* (University of Arizona Press, 2003)

Martin Espada's *The Republic of Poetry* (W.W. Norton, 2006)

Tim Z. Hernández's *Skin Tax* (Heyday Books, 2005)

Juan Felipe Herrera's *187 Reasons Mexicanos Can't Cross the Border* (City Lights Books, 2008)

Sheryl Luna's *Pity the Drowned Horses* (University of Notre Dame Press, 2005)

Valerie Martínez's *Each and Her* (University of Arizona Press, 2010)

Maria Meléndez's *How Long She'll Last in This World* (University of Arizona Press, 2006)

John Murillo's *Up Jump the Boogie* (Cypher Books, 2010)

Benjamin Alire Sáenz's *Dreaming the End of War* (Copper Canyon Press, 2006)

Some thoughts: I wouldn't argue with the selection of any of these books. The work of each of these poets is integral to the issues being discussed in contemporary Latinx verse. Here are some things I especially like about this roster: the overwhelming nod towards small and university presses; *Up Jump the Boogie*'s inclusion, not only because it was one of the best books of poetry that year (2010), but as a nod to the increasing and merited attention to Afro-Latinx poetics; that seven of the twelve titles are first books; (on a personal note) that four of the twelve poets appeared in *The Wind Shifts* anthology I edited.

And yet, I *do* question, in the context of *Pivotal Voices*, the inclusion of Francisco X. Alarcón and Juan Felipe Herrera. Here's why: González already includes a fine twelve-page study that engages five books, titled "Juan Felipe Herrera's Global Voice and Vision," which concludes this second section; he also already includes a moving fifteen-page study which concludes section three and the book itself, titled "Erotic Light, Amor Oscuro: On the Queer Poetics of Francisco X. Alarcón and his Muse, Federico Garcia Lorca." Given, therefore, that *Pivotal Voices* already devotes ample space, and rigorously so, to Herrera and Alarcón, respectively: why not a more gender-balanced, twelve-part piece that treats six male poets and six female poets (instead of this eight men/four women break-down)?

That said, in piece after piece—one through twelve—González's mastery of the 500-word review is on full display: the way he skillfully conveys a succinct "plot summary" of the collection in question, his knack for seamlessly weaving poetic fragments into the argument of his narrative, and his occasional citations of whole stand-alone passages—always carefully curated to pack a punch. Here he is on Brenda Cárdenas' *Boomerang*:

> From this childhood appreciation of culture and an early affinity for linguistic play rises the mature voice of a strong woman who sings the praises of el mestizaje ('if you can't dig la mezcla, chale!'), who can chew on a poem in Old English and spit it back out in Old Chicano English ('Language lies / across the barbed lines'), and who wistfully pronounces, 'We work in English / make love in Spanish / and code-switch past our indecision.'

Or this passage on *How Long She'll Last in This World*:

> Meléndez contends that violence and healing are base pairs to this dark but glorious age. Humanity and nature are its co-habitants. And so this challenge: 'There is a time to grip your talismans, a time to strip yourself of them.' The speaker asks us to reconnect to 'these places you never left' and recognize that 'more lives move beside us than we know.' From these important gestures, the recovery of memory and spiritual-ecological health begins.

Before the publication of *How Long She'll Last in This World*, Meléndez had published a chapbook with Sandra McPherson's Swan Scythe Press. Its title? You guessed it: *Base Pairs*. Coincidence, or intentional, on González's part ("violence and healing are base pairs")? Doesn't matter. The effect is the same on this reader, and others with this shared tidbit of Meléndez's publication history: it's an added, nuanced, layer of engagement and pleasure.

I had mentioned "Juan Felipe Herrera's Global Voice and Vision" as the piece that closes section two of the book. It's something of an anomaly: it's the only piece in this section that deals with a single author. This second section is dominated by pieces that take on multiple poets, such as the twelve-poet configuration just discussed. The opening piece in section two ("Publishers on a Mission: Three Excellent Debut Poets") adopts the added agenda of highlighting three book prizes that aim to ensure diversity in publishing. González offers substantive commentary on Laurie Ann Guerrero's *A Tongue in the Mouth of the Dying* (University of Notre Dame Press, 2013), winner of the Andrés Montoya Poetry Prize; Matthew Olzmann's *Mezzanines* (Alice James Books, 2013), winner of the Kundiman Poetry Prize; and L. Lamar Wilson's *Sacrilegion* (Carolina Wren Press, 2013), a product of the Carolina Wren Poetry Series, whose mission is to publish "quality writing, especially by writers ignored by mainstream publishing." Another piece in section two highlights three first books by African American poets: Jamaal May, Kamilah Aisha Moon, and Roger Reeves. Rigoberto González also takes on the laudable task of examining the work of three more-established poets in "Midcareer: Three Poets and their Four Books." The individuals he's selected for this distinction are Quan Barry, Kyle Dargan, and Ada Limón. Of all the pieces in *Pivotal Voices*, this was the least satisfying. The strategy of discussing four distinct books by each of the three poets felt, in the end, like too ambitious an approach. I didn't get as good a feel for each volume of poetry as I did everywhere else in *Pivotal Voices*. I suspect this was the case because of the necessary space restrictions given the number of books to be treated in a single piece. An alternative approach—albeit probably more ambitious but in a different sense—would have been to identify and examine a particular topic (one per poet) and discuss a poem from each of the poets' four books—through the lens of their respective topics.

The piece from this section, on the other hand, that captivated me was "On *Karankawa* and *The Animal Too Big to Kill*." We learn, in the publications acknowledgements, that the treatment of these two books were each published separately in *The Rumpus*. But something about intentionally placing them side by side in one piece was, curatorially speaking, genius. They are both books that deal, on some level, with challenging family relationships and legacies, and that may be the secret sauce I was tasting by reading these reviews back to back, as González intended. And, as circumstances would have it, both Iliana Rocha (*Karankawa*) and Shane McCrae (*The Animal Too Big to Kill*) are poets I knew by name, but not overly familiar with their work. González's twin reviews will result in my actively seeking out these two books. His brilliantly proportioned alchemy of citation, analysis, and plot summary have, once again, done the trick of making a reader want to track the titles down.

III

Critical Grace Notes

In his brief preface to the third and final section of *Pivotal Voices*, Rigoberto González writes: "I believe it was Gloria Anzaldúa who encouraged queer and feminist critics to write the self in the work . . ." This statement is related to why, after reading this section, I felt prompted to think: *Pivotal Voices* should be required reading for anyone enrolled in a graduate creative writing program. The texts, in particular, that spur me to articulate this are a keynote address ("The Activist Role of the Writer"), a commencement address ("The Writer's Journey: A Motivation"), and an acceptance speech ("Bill Whitehead Award for Lifetime Achievement Speech"). The first is a moving, at times heartbreaking testimonial of González's journey of coming into his queer identity within a challenging family dynamic. At one point, in discussing the less-than-accepting environment he was raised in, he resorts to the third person:

> It seemed that even his facial features gave him away. All the other boy faces in his family were pure muscle and bone, while his was so awkwardly doughy and rosy, a ripe plum in a bowl of potatoes. And if that wasn't enough, when he walked into the room he brought along a pronounced lisp like a pink balloon. What other recourse for self-preservation but staying still and quiet, what other way to survive but by becoming a near absence in the house, an errant puddle near the wall that each day receded more?

That image of the receding puddle is a metaphor: the boy is slowly dying on the inside. The piece is also about how discovering queer and Latinx literature, and writing, saved him:

> This journey is my life, and it's personal, and it's the reason I became a writer: to add to those bookshelves that not only shape lives, they save them. What more noble cause than that, than to save the lives of our youth? And perhaps I'm saving myself each time I complete a book and toss it out to the sea of readers like a life preserver. *Someone* will grab it—grab hold of me.

I could cite more passages from the commencement and acceptance speech to similar effect, but I think these suffice to convey why these testimonials gave the book what I'll call its "handbook feel." I would have loved holding a volume like this in my hands twenty years ago while pursuing my creative writing MA and MFA. *Pivotal Voices* could, today, with the right frame of mind, be a guidebook on cultivating one's aspiration to be a poet-critic (sections I & II), and/or a poet-thinker (section III) . . . *if* one is open to the challenge—*to the measure and degree that suits one.* González seems to express some rigidity on this score. At the end of his brief preface to section two he writes:

> My only disappointment after I left the El Paso Times was that no oth-
> er Latino writer took the opportunity to replace me. A few attempts
> were made but none of the would-be columnists achieved my level of
> production or discipline. This many years later, I'm still waiting for
> someone else to make such a commitment in service to the Latino
> writing community.

How he deploys "my level" and "such a" in the above passage seems to turn a momentary blind eye on the notion that Latinx writers—not a homogenous group to begin with—bring different proclivities and abilities to their re-spective "service" to the Latinx writing community, or whatever other com-munity they serve—as well as different life trajectories, which can translate into different motivations and priorities. In contrast, González is firmly on the mark in "The Writer's Journey: A Motivation," the commencement speech in section three, when he writes: "[S]ometimes that means the writ-ing will take place slowly—and that's all right, writing's not a race." The cliché, with a twist, is useful here: one size does *not* fit all.

Rigoberto González and I share something: we were both formally men-tored by the late Francisco X. Alarcón—he sat on each of our respective MA thesis committees at UC Davis. In the days after Alarcón died in January of 2016, we reached out to one another to share stories of our time with him at Davis. Although I'd known Alarcón since the mid 1980s, mainly in my ca-pacity as his translator, it was from a distance. The relationship unfurled fully during my two years in Davis (1998–2000), as it did for González during his stint there (1992–1994). Shortly after his death, I wrote my tribute to Fran-cisco at Letras Latinas Blog ("Francisco X. Alarcón: tocayo") and González wrote his at NBC Latino ("Voices: Remembering Friend, Mentor and Poet Francisco X. Alarcón"), which serves as the first section of "Erotic Light, Amor Oscuro: On the Queer Poetics of Francisco X. Alarcón and His Muse,

Federico García Lorca"—the final essay in *Pivotal Voices*. I provided some of the background for it—as it pertains to Alarcón's homoerotic sonnet collection, *De Amor Oscuro/Of Dark Love*, which I translated into English. And I also appear in the piece itself, as the person who made Alarcón aware of Lorca's homoerotic sonnet sequence, "Sonetos del amor oscuro."

What I can say is this: considering the fact that one of Rigoberto González's touchstone principals as a thinker is his insistence on fully embodying and articulating his twin identities as Chicano and gay, and therefore a gay Chicano artist, it's not at all surprising that he would reserve the final slot in *Pivotal Voices* for the mentor who most instilled in him this principal. So while it might make more logical sense for the essay on Alarcón to reside in section one of this book, "Critical Essays," having it in section three, "Critical Grace Notes," makes perfect sense, and is more in line with the notion of writing the self into the work—that is, a more personal gesture with more at stake. It also allows the book's "farewell" to the reader to also serve as González's final "farewell" to Alarcón. González even opts for the personal in his farewell to the reader to end the essay and the book:

> And so I end with this appeal: when I die, talk about my work, talk about my activism, talk about how much I cared about my communities, but don't silence the part of my identity that walked every single step along with me to the rally, the classroom, the desk, the podium, that part of my identity that makes me susceptible to hatred and fear and ignorance and hurt. That part of me I also appreciate and love, and so should you.

He's alluding to being gay, and this closing passage of the essay harkens back to an earlier passage of the piece:

> When Francisco agreed to sit on my thesis committee, I began to consider seriously the term *Chicano*—something I had resisted because I had always called myself Mexican. I didn't know I could inhabit all of

these identities at once until I met Francisco, who embodied many of them. Like him, I had been born in the United States and spent my childhood in Mexico. Like him, I was bilingual, bicultural, and gay.

In the end, *Pivotal Voices, Era of Transition: Towards a 21st Century Poetics* stands *in* for Rigoberto González's cumulative achievement(s) as a critic and thinker. It also stands firmly *beside* his achievement(s) as a multi-genre artist of his own literary work—twin monuments.

January 2018
Torquay, England
Works Cited

González, Rigoberto. *Pivotal Voices, Era of Transition: Towards a 21st Century Poetics*. Ann Arbor, Michigan. University of Michigan Press, 2017.

González, Rigoberto. *Red-Inked Retablos*. Tucson, Arizona. University of Arizona Press, 2013.

REVIEWS

Contributor
Notes

Samuel Ace

Anna Akhmatova

Francisco Aragón

Anna Augustyniak

Justyna Bargielska

Polina Barskova

Heather Bartlett

Curtis Bauer

Renée Branum

Anders Carlson-Wee

Kai Carlson-Wee

Mark Cassidy

Victoria Chang

Leila Chatti

Steven Cordova

Debra A. Daniel

Kendra DeColo

Chelsea Dingman

Jehanne Dubrow

Kathy Fagan

Ashley Farmer

Katie Farris

Sonia Feigelson

Katie Ford

Gina Franco

Sonia Greenfield

Joseph Hernandez

Maria Jastrzębska

Ilya Kaminsky

Joseph Lapin

Ilya Leybovich

Sabrina Li

Margaret Mackinnon

Maija Mäkinen

Carol D. Marsh

LaTanya McQueen

Jen Palmares Meadows

Fabio Morábito

Susannah Nevison

Samantha Niedzielski

Catherine Pierce

Carol Potter

Wesley Rothman

Anne Royan

Anja Snellman

Danusia Stok

Donley Watt

Zach Weber

Allison Benis White

Sherraine Pate Williams

SAMUEL ACE is a genderqueer poet, sound artist, photographer, and teacher. He has published three collections of poetry: *Normal Sex, Home in Three Days, Don't Wash*, and most recently *Stealth*, with poet Maureen Seaton. He is a recipient of a New York Foundation for the Arts fellowship, two-time finalist for Lambda Literary Award in Poetry, winner of the Astraea Lesbian Writers Fund Award in Poetry, the Katherine Anne Porter Prize for Fiction, and the Firecracker Alternative Book Award in poetry. He was also recent finalist for the National Poetry Series. His work has been widely anthologized and has appeared in or is forthcoming from *Fence, Vinyl, Plume, Aufgabe, Atlas Review, Mandorla, Volt, Ploughshares, Eoagh, Spiral Orb, Kenyon Review, Everyday Genius, Rhino, 3:am, Versal, Trickhouse, The Collagist, Eleven Eleven, Tupelo Quarterly, The Volta, Devouring the Green, Troubling the Line: Genderqueer Poetry and Poetics*, and *Best American Experimental Poetry 2016*. He lives in Tucson, Arizona, and is currently a Visiting Lecturer in Creative Writing at Mount Holyoke College in South Hadley, Massachusetts. His work can be found at www.samuelace.com.

Born in Odessa, ANNA AKHMATOVA is one of the four most important Russian poets of the twentieth century, others being Mandelstam, Tsvetaeva, and Pasternak. She was associated with Akhmeism movement.

A San Francisco native, FRANCISCO ARAGÓN is the son of Nicaraguan immigrants. Upon his return to the U.S. in 1998 after a decade in Spain, Aragón completed graduate degrees in creative writing from UC Davis and the University of Notre Dame. In 2003 he joined the faculty of Notre Dame's Institute for Latino Studies, where he established Letras Latinas. In 2017, he was a finalist for Split This Rock's Freedom Plow Award for poetry and activism. A CantoMundo fellow and a member of the Macondo Writers' Workshop, he is the author of two books: *Puerta del Sol* and *Glow of Our Sweat*, as well as editor of the anthology: *The Wind Shifts: New Latino Poetry*. He is currently completing a third book, *After Rubén*.

ANNA AUGUSTYNIAK is a prolific print and radio journalist, biographer, and poet. Among her many awards and honors are the 2015 "Złoty Środek Poezji" award for the best poetic debut of the year and a fellowship from the Polish Ministry of Culture and National Heritage. Her poetry, fiction, and nonfiction have been translated into Romanian, Russian, Serbian, Spanish, Ukrainian, Hebrew, Turkish, Belarusian, Slovenian, and German. Anna Augustyniak lives in Warsaw, Poland.

Born in Warsaw in 1977, JUSTYNA BARGIELSKA has published eight poetry collections, two works of fiction, two children's books, and two plays. She is twice winner of the Gdynia Literary Prize—in 2010 for her poetry collection *Dwa fiaty* (Two Fiats) and in 2011 for her short fiction, *Obsoletki* (Born Sleeping)—and, among many other awards, winner of the Rainer Maria Rilke poetry competition in 2001. Her collection Selfie na tle rzepaka (Selfie against a field of rape) is from Biuro Literackie, 2016. A literary drama *Clarissima* was premiered in Zakopane in 2014. Her work has been translated into French, German, Slovene, Dutch, Russian, and Czech. She lives in Warsaw and teaches at the Jagiellonian University in Kraków. *The Great Plan B*, selected poems by Justyna Bargielska translated from Polish by Maria Jastrzębska, is from Smokestack Press 2017.

Born in St. Petersburg, POLINA BARSKOVA is a contemporary Russian poet, author of many acclaimed books of verse, including *Euridis* and *Orphica*.

HEATHER BARTLETT holds an MFA in poetry from Hunter College. Her recent work can be found in *Barrow Street, Carolina Quarterly, Nimrod, Ninth Letter, PoemMemoirStory,* and other journals. A lecturer in English at the State University of New York at Cortland, she lives, writes, and grades papers in Ithaca, New York.

CURTIS BAUER is a poet (most recently *The Real Cause for Your Absence* [C&R Press]) and a translator of poetry and prose from the Spanish (most recently *Eros Is More*, by Juan Antonio González Iglesias [Alice James Books] & *From Behind What Landscape*, by Luis Muñoz [Vaso Roto Editions]). He teaches creative writing and comparative literature at Texas Tech University.

RENÉE BRANUM currently lives and works in Missoula. She recently graduated with an MFA in Creative Nonfiction from the University of Montana. She received an MFA in Fiction from the Iowa Writers' Workshop in 2013. Renée's fiction has appeared in *Blackbird* and *The Long Story*, with stories forthcoming in the *Georgia Review, Tampa Review, Narrative Magazine,* and *Alaska Quarterly Review.* Her nonfiction essays have been published or are forthcoming in *Fields Magazine, Texas Review, True Story, Denver Quarterly,* and *Chicago Quarterly Review.*

ANDERS CARLSON-WEE is the author of *The Low Passions* (W.W. Norton, 2019). He has received fellowships from the NEA, the McKnight Foundation, Bread Loaf, the Sewanee Writers' Conference, and the Napa Valley Writers' Conference. His work has appeared in *The Nation, The Kenyon Review, BuzzFeed, Ploughshares, New England Review, Poetry Daily, The Sun,* and *The Best American Nonrequired Reading.* His debut chapbook, *Dynamite,* won the 2015 Frost Place Chapbook Prize. He is codirector of the award-winning poetry film, *Riding the Highline,* and his work has been translated into Chinese. Winner of *Ninth Letter*'s Poetry Award, *Blue Mesa Review*'s Poetry Prize, *New Delta Review*'s Editors' Choice Prize, and the 2017 *Poetry International Prize,* he lives in Minneapolis.

KAI CARLSON-WEE is the author of *RAIL* (BOA Editions, 2018). He has received fellowships from the MacDowell Colony, the Bread Loaf Writers Conference, the Sewanee Writers Conference, and his work appears in *Ploughshares, Best New Poets, New England Review, Gulf Coast,* and the *Missouri Review,* which awarded him the 2013 Editor's Prize. His photography has been featured in *Narrative Magazine* and his poetry film, *Riding the Highline,* received jury awards at the 2015 Napa Valley Film Festival and the

2016 Arizona International Film Festival. A former Wallace Stegner Fellow, he lives in San Francisco and is a lecturer at Stanford University.

MARK CASSIDY was born in Scotland, considers Canada home and presently lives in Houston. He has lived and worked in various locales around the world, including West Africa, out of which the two stories here emerged. He has had several short stories and flash pieces published both in the US and the UK.

VICTORIA CHANG's fourth book of poems, *Barbie Chang*, was published in 2017 by Copper Canyon Press. *The Boss* (McSweeney's) won the PEN Center USA Literary Award and a California Book Award. Her other books are *Salvinia Molesta* and *Circle*. She was awarded a Guggenheim Fellowship and a Sustainable Arts Foundation Fellowship in 2017. She serves as Teaching Faculty at Antioch's MFA Program in Los Angeles and also serves on the National Book Critics Circle Board. You can find her at www.victoriachangpoet.com.

LEILA CHATTI is a Tunisian-American poet and author of the chapbooks *Ebb* and *Tunsiya/Amrikiya*. A recipient of fellowships from the Fine Arts Work Center in Provincetown, the *Tin House* Writers' Workshop, and the Wisconsin Institute for Creative Writing, her poems appear in *Ploughshares*, *Tin House*, *Virginia Quarterly Review*, *The Rumpus*, and elsewhere.

STEVEN CORDOVA's full-length collection of poetry, *Long Distance*, was published by Bilingual Review Press in 2010. His poems have appeared in *Barrow Street*, *Bellevue Literary Review*, *Callaloo*, *The Journal*, and *Northwest Review*. He reviews fiction and nonfiction for Lambda Literary. From San Antonio, Texas, he lives in Brooklyn, New York.

DEBRA A. DANIEL is the author of the novel *Woman Commits Suicide in Dishwasher* (Muddy Ford Press) and poetry chapbooks *The Downward Turn of*

August (Finishing Line Press) and *As Is* (Main Street Rag). She was twice named SC Arts Commission Poetry Fellow, won the Guy Owen Prize, and was a Pushcart nominee. Her work has appeared in such places as *Jasper Magazine, Smokelong Quarterly, darkskymagazine.com, Kakalak, Emrys Journal, Pequin.org, Inkwell, Southern Poetry Review, Tar River,* and *Gargoyle*. She lives in Columbia, South Carolina, with her musician husband with whom she sings and plays cardboard box percussion in an eclectic acoustic band.

KENDRA DECOLO is the author of *My Dinner with Ron Jeremy* (Third Man Books, 2016) and *Thieves in the Afterlife* (Saturnalia Books, 2014), selected by Yusef Komunyakaa for the 2013 Saturnalia Books Poetry Prize. Her poems and essays have appeared or are forthcoming in *Gulf Coast, Ninth Letter, Bitch Magazine, VIDA, Verse Daily,* and elsewhere. She has received awards and fellowships from the MacDowell Colony, the Bread Loaf Writers Conference, the Millay Colony and the Tennessee Arts Commission. She lives in Nashville, Tennessee.

CHELSEA DINGMAN's first book, *Thaw*, was chosen by Allison Joseph to win the National Poetry Series (2017). She recently won the *Southeast Review*'s Gearhart Poetry Prize, the *Sycamore Review*'s Wabash Prize, and *Water-Stone Review*'s Jane Kenyon Poetry Prize. She has work in *Ninth Letter, The Colorado Review,* and *Gulf Coast*. www.chelseadingman.com.

JEHANNE DUBROW is the author of six poetry collections, including most recently *Dots & Dashes*, winner of the Crab Orchard Series in Poetry Open Competition Award. Her work has appeared in *Pleiades, New England Review,* and *Southern Review*. She is an associate professor at the University of North Texas.

KATHY FAGAN's newest collection is *Sycamore* (Milkweed Editions, 2017). A recipient of NEA and OAC fellowships, her recent work appears in *Poetry,*

Numero Cinq, The New Republic, Blackbird, and *Crazyhorse.* Fagan directs the MFA Program at Ohio State and edits the *OSU Press/The Journal Wheeler* Poetry Prize Series.

ASHLEY FARMER is the author of the collections *The Women* (Civil Coping Mechanisms, 2016), *The Farmacist* (Jellyfish Highway Press, 2015), *Beside Myself* (PANK/Tiny Hardcore Press, 2014), and the chapbook *Farm Town* (Rust Belt Bindery, 2012). A recipient of fellowships from Syracuse University and the Baltic Writing Residency, her work can be found in places like *Santa Monica Review, The Collagist, Buzzfeed, Gigantic, The Progressive, Nerve,* and *Flaunt.* Ashley lives in Salt Lake City, Utah, and serves as a fiction editor for Juked.

KATIE FARRIS is the author of *boysgirls* (Marick Press) and co-editor of *Gossip and Metaphysics: Russian Modernist Poems & Prose* (Tupelo Press). She teaches in the MFA program at SDSU.

SONIA FEIGELSON is a Brooklyn-based writer and actress. Her work can be seen in or is forthcoming from *Split Lip Magazine, Two Serious Ladies, Burrow Press Review, Temenos, Extract(s),* and *Quaint,* among others. She was a 2010 recipient of the Memoir award from Random House Creative Writing Competition. Most recently, she was awarded third prize in *Glimmer Train*'s Short Story Award for New Writers. She has only ever kept one plant alive. www.twitter.com/FeigelsonSonia.

KATIE FORD is the author of *Deposition, Colosseum,* and *Blood Lyrics,* which was a finalist for the LA Times Book Prize and the Rilke Prize. *Colosseum* was named among the "Best Books of 2008" by *Publishers Weekly* and the *Virginia Quarterly Review* and led to a Lannan Literary Fellowship and the Larry Levis Prize. The *New Yorker,* the *Norton Introduction to Literature, Poetry Magazine,* the *Paris Review,* and the *American Poetry Review* have published her poems. She served as a 2016 judge for the National Book

Award in Poetry. Her next book, *If You Have To Go*, will be published by Graywolf Press in August 2018. She is Professor of Creative Writing and Director of the MFA Program at the University of California, Riverside.

GINA FRANCO is the author of *The Keepsake Storm*. Her work has appeared in many journals, including *32 Poems, Black Warrior Review, BorderSenses, Copper Nickel, Crazyhorse, Diagram, Image: Art, Faith, Mystery, Fence*, the *Georgia Review, Poetry, Tuesday; an Art Project, West Branch Wired*, and *Zone 3*. Her writing is also anthologized in *A Best of Fence: the First Nine Years, The Wind Shifts: New Latino Poetry, Camino del Sol: Fifteen Years of Latina and Latino Writing*, and *The Other Latin@: Writing Against a Singular Identity*. She is an oblate with the Catholic monastic order of the Community of Saint John, and she teaches at Knox College in Galesburg, Illinois.

SONIA GREENFIELD is the author of two books of poems: *American Parable* (Autumn House) and *Boy With a Halo at the Farmer's Market* (Codhill Press). Her work has appeared or is forthcoming in the 2018 and 2010 *Best American Poetry, Antioch Review, Bellevue Literary Review, Massachusetts Review*, and *Willow Springs*, among others. Her collection of prose poems, *Letdown*, is forthcoming in 2020 with White Pine Press as part of the Marie Alexander Series. She lives with her husband and son in Hollywood where she edits the *Rise Up Review* and directs the Southern California Poetry Festival.

JOSEPH HERNANDEZ is a Southern California native whose fiction has explored the dynamics of families, fruit trees, and mermaids. He received his MFA from California State University, Long Beach, and currently teaches Critical Thinking in Writing courses at the college level.

MARIA JASTRZĘBSKA was born in Warsaw and came to the UK as a child. She co-translated *Elsewhere,* the selected poems of Iztok Osojnik with Ana Jelnikar (Pighog Press 2011). Her translation of an extract of Justyna Bargielska's *Obsoletki* (*Born Sleeping*) featured in *Best European Fiction* (Dalkey Archive 2016). Her most recent collection was *At The Library of Memories* (Waterloo Press 2013) and her selected poems *The Cedars of Walpole Park* were translated into Polish by Wioletta Grzegorzewska, Anna Błasiak and Paweł Gawroński (Stowarzyszenie Żywych Poetów 2015). A new work *The True Story of Cowboy Hat and Ingénue* is forthcoming in 2018.

ILYA KAMINSKY was born in Odessa, Ukraine, and currently lives in San Diego.

JOSEPH LAPIN is a storyteller, journalist, author, creative director, and photographer living in San Diego, California. His writing has appeared at the *Los Angeles Times*, the *Village Voice*, *LA Weekly*, *Narratively*, *The Rattling Wall*, and *Huck Magazine*. He is the host and creator of *The Working Poet Radio Show*, a podcast and live show sponsored by the Miami Book Fair dedicated to the working lives of creative people. He is currently the creative director at Circa Interactive.

ILYA LEYBOVICH's fiction has appeared in *St. Ann's Review*, *Chicago Quarterly Review*, *Fiction International*, *deComp*, *Little Patuxent Review*, *Notre Dame Review*, and *Southern California Review*. He lives in Brooklyn, New York.

SABRINA LI is a current sophomore at Harvard College. She is the head features editor of the *Harvard Advocate* and works at PEN America's Artists At Risk Connection. She's passionate about fighting for human rights and artistic expression. Her fiction has appeared in the *Harvard Advocate*, *On The Rusk*, and the *Claremont Review*.

MARGARET MACKINNON's work has appeared in *Poetry*, *Image*, *Shenandoah*, and other journals. Her first book, *The Invented Child*, won the Gerald Cable Book Award and the Literary Award in Poetry from the Library of Virginia. A chapbook, *Naming the Natural World*, is forthcoming in 2018.

MAIJA MÄKINEN is a Finnish-born writer and translator with an MFA in Fiction from Boston University. Her writings and translations have been featured or are forthcoming in *Gulf Coast*, *Transnational Literature*, and *Best New Writing*, among others. She is the winner of the University of Cambridge Lucy Cavendish Fiction Prize.

CAROL D. MARSH is an award-winning essayist and author of the recently released memoir, *Nowhere Else I Want to Be*. A 2014 graduate of the MFA-CNF program at Goucher College, she's won awards from *New Millennium Writings*, *under the gum tree*, and *Soundings Review*. www.caroldmarsh.com.

LATANYA MCQUEEN has most recently been published in *Indiana Review*, *Passages North*, *Bennington Review*, *Ninth Letter*, *Carve Magazine*, and *Harpur Palate*. She received her MFA from Emerson College and is finishing her PhD at the University of Missouri.

JEN PALMARES MEADOWS is a Pinay American essayist living in the Sacramento, California area. Her writing has appeared in *The Rumpus*, *Brevity*, *Fourth Genre*, *Denver Quarterly*, *The Nervous Breakdown*, *Quarter After Eight*, *Essay Daily*, and elsewhere.

FABIO MORÁBITO was born in Alexandria, Egypt, in 1955 to Italian parents. He moved to Milan when he was five, and when he was fifteen he moved to Mexico City, where he currently lives and works in the Autonomous University of Mexico. Morábito is the author of four books of poetry (including *De lunes todo el año* [1992] [*Monday All Year Long*], which won the Aguascalientes National Poetry Prize, and *Delante de un prado una vaca* [*In Front of a Pasture, a Cow*] [Visor, 2013]), two novels (including *Caja de herramientas* [*Tool Box*] [Fondo de Cultura Económica, 1989], which was translated into English by Geoff Hargreaves and published by Xenox Books in 1996), five books of short stories (including *La vida ordenada* [*An Ordered Life*] (Tusquets, 2000) and *Grieta de fatiga* [*Rift of Fatigue*] [Tusquets,

2012]), and three books of essays (including *El idioma materno* [*Mother Tongue*] [Sexto Piso, 2014]). Morábito is also a prolific translator, and he has translated the complete works of Eugenio Montale and Aminto de Torquato Tasso, among many other Italian poets and prose writers. In addition to Geoff Hargreaves's English translation of the book *Tool Box*, his writing has been translated into German, French, Portuguese, and Italian.

SUSANNAH NEVISON is the author of *Teratology* (Persea Books, 2015), winner of the Lexi Rudnitsky First Book Prize in Poetry. New work can be found in, or is forthcoming from, *Crazyhorse*, the *National Poetry Review*, *Guernica*, and elsewhere. She is a 2016 Clarence Snow Fellow and doctoral candidate at the University of Utah. Her second book, *Lethal Theater*, won the 2018 Wheeler Prize and is forthcoming from OSU in 2019.

Mexican-American poet and painter SAMANTHA NIEDZIELSKI was born in Atlanta, Georgia. She since then has lived in Ohio, California, and Mexico. Her work combines memoir, geography, and observation. She has studied with Marty McConnell, Junse Kim, and Kim Addonizio, and is currently working as a bookseller in Berkeley, California, while writing her first collection of poetry.

CATHERINE PIERCE's most recent book of poems is *The Tornado Is the World* (Saturnalia 2016); her other books are *The Girls of Peculiar* (2012) and *Famous Last Words* (2008). Her work has appeared in the *Best American Poetry*, *Ploughshares*, *Boston Review*, the *Southern Review*, and elsewhere. She co-directs the creative writing program at Mississippi State University.

CAROL POTTER is the 2014 winner of the *Field Poetry* Prize for her fifth book of poems, *Some Slow Bees* from Oberlin College Press. Potter's poems have appeared in *Green Mountains Review*, *Field*, the *Iowa Review*, *Poetry*, the *American Poetry Review*, the *Kenyon Review*, and many other journals and anthologies. She has recent poems in *Hotel Amerika*, the *Massachusetts Re-*

view, and the *New England Review*, and poems forthcoming in *River Styx*, *Field*, and *Poet Lore*. She teaches for the Antioch University MFA program in Los Angeles. cwpotterverse.net

WESLEY ROTHMAN is the author of *SUBWOOFER* (New Issues, 2017). His poems and criticism have appeared in *Boston Review*, *Callaloo*, *Crazyhorse*, *Gulf Coast*, *New England Review*, *Publishers Weekly*, and the *Golden Shovel Anthology*, among other venues. Recipient of a Vermont Studio Center Fellowship, he serves as a Teaching Artist for the National Gallery of Art and lives in Washington, DC.

ANNE ROYAN is a graduate of Savannah College of Art & Design (MFA, Writing), Brown University (BA) and the Columbia Publishing Course at Columbia University. She has worked in the fashion department at Harper's Bazaar in New York City and as a PR Director for jewelry brands. She is a freelance contributing writer for magazines. A recipient of a SCAD Alumni Atelier Ambassadorship, she is at work on a series of travel essays in Provence, France.

ANJA SNELLMAN (Kauranen until 1997), born in 1954, is one of the leading figures in Finnish literature and rose to fame with her debut novel *Sonja O. Was Here*. She has published more than twenty novels and several collections of poetry, and her works have been translated into more than twenty languages. In addition to writing, Snellman also works as a therapist for young people in a Helsinki detox program.

DANUSIA STOK was born and educated in England. She is the editor of *Kieslowski on Kieslowski*, and has translated, among other authors, *The Trilogy* by K. Kieslowski and K. Piesiewicz, *I Remember Nothing More* by Adina Blady-Szwajger, *The Journals of a White Sea Wolf* by Mariusz Wilk, *The Witcher* and *The Blood of Elves* by Andrzej Sapkowski, *Death in Breslau*, *The End of the World in Breslau*, *Phantoms of Breslau* and *The Head of the*

Minotaur by Marek Krajewski, *Illegal Liaisons* by Grażyna Plebanek, and *Polichrome* by Joanna Jodełka.

DONLEY WATT lives in Santa Fe, New Mexico. His collection of short stories, *Can You Get There from Here?*, won the Texas Institute of Letters' prize for best first book of fiction. Since then he has had four more book-length works of fiction published, along with many other stories and essays.

ZACH WEBER is a twenty-three-year-old poet and writer. He is a high school dropout. He never knows what to write for his author bio. He loves you.

ALLISON BENIS WHITE is the author of *Please Bury Me in This* (2017) and *Small Porcelain Head* (2013), selected by Claudia Rankine for the Levis Prize. Her first book, *Self-Portrait with Crayon* (2009), received the Cleveland State University Poetry Center Book Prize. She teaches at the University of California, Riverside.

SHERRAINE PATE WILLIAMS's most recently published poems have appeared in *Southern Poetry Review*, the *Los Angles Review*, *Mezzo Cammin*, and elsewhere. She holds an MFA in poetry from Murray State University's creative writing program and teaches basic literacy skills to adults. She currently lives in Kentucky with her family.

www.ingramcontent.com/pod-product-compliance
Lightning Source LLC
Chambersburg PA
CBHW031951010726
47493CB00007B/2165